Unlawful Love

Our Love is Justified

By:

Chey

Legal Notes

Synopsis

First story, IN HOUSE WAR is where you meet Marque, a two time veteran who resides in a small town in Massachusetts. He has a crazy ex, a new love and a racist cop ... Put it all together and he is victimized and shot by a cop but he ends up being the one charged.

Second story, RUNNIN' is where you meet Lynique who ran away from home and boyfriend five years ago after being fed up having hands put on her, when she ran off she left with a secret that's revealed when she returns. Falling back in love with your former abuser is a risk she decided to take.

Find out what destiny has in store for Marque and Lynique by getting your copy of:
Unlawful Love, Our Love is Justified.

Table of Contents

In House War

1994

"*Please Mack stop, I'm sorry but don't hit me again. Look at what you did to my face already. Marque is awake in the other room, he can't see this. Think about him for once if not me.*" *I could hear my mother begging my father to stop another beat down. She didn't know because I never said anything about it, but this wasn't the first time I have heard the screams and assaults. It has become normal to be woken up while daddy dearest stumbles into our run-down trailer drunk after spending his pay check at the bar. This specific time his reasoning is because my mother had made BBQ chicken and not fried. He would look for a reason, I mean walk around the house looking for something small, so he could knock her around. He knew she didn't have anyone. He made sure of that when he made her move away from her disapproving family. I guess my papa could tell Mack was a ain't shit man who wasn't going to amount to shit but being naïve and in love, my mother chose to leave and along came me. 15 years later and I'm laying here fist clenched tired of hearing her pleading and apologizing when she did nothing wrong.*

Not able to lay here and do nothing any longer, I decided to get up and put a stop to it. My queen did nothing wrong. It was going to stop tonight if I had anything to do with it. Walking to my closet to grab my Louisville slugger I had gotten a few years back when I played baseball, I knew I was going to need something to face off with my father. He wasn't a small man at all. He was 6'3 and 260 solid. He worked in a warehouse loading and unloading trucks all day lifting heavy ass boxes.

Walking down the small narrow hall quietly not wanting to alarm them that I was up and moving around, I stopped outside of the door to the bedroom they shared. I could hear my mother gasping for air and what sounding like something thumping against the wall, the headboard maybe. Not sure what I was going to walk into but knowing I was fed up, I barged in and I am so thankful I did. This asshole who went half on creating me was on top of my mother with his hands wrapped around her throat while pumping ferociously into her ass. I could see blood leaking from somewhere. I just swung the bat with all my might and cracked my father in the head. Seeing now the bruises, new and old that my mother has done good hiding on her body with clothing enraged me. I stood over my now unconscious piece of shit dad and raised the bat and just kept striking him over and over.

Finally dropping the bat, I walked over and covered my mother with a sheet and went to call 911. She wasn't moving but I could tell she was still alive and needed help. I was prepared to go to jail for hurting my father, I just hope my mother leaves him because if not she was as good as dead. I walked to the kitchen and picked up the phone.

"911 What's your emergency?"

"Yes, please send help. My father hurt my mother and she isn't getting up, I also hurt my father because of it and he's bleeding pretty bad. Just send someone quick. The address is 1694 Scottsdale Rd."

I had hung up the phone and rushed back to check on my mother. She was looking around and once our eyes met she asked me why. I was confused on what she meant. I hoped she wasn't upset that I put an end to her being a *punching bag.*

"Why what Ma?"

"Why did you come in here? Marque why did you hurt him! Look what you did he's not breathing, you killed your father. You took him from me WHY DAMMIT WHY COULDN'T YOU JUST HAVE STAYED IN YOUR ROOM!"

Was I hearing her correctly? Was she really mad at me for protecting her? She almost died at the hands of that man, he was raping her, and she didn't even care. Are these people even my parents because ain't no way I'm a product of these two?

BANG BANG BANG "Open the door"

I walked out to let the cops and paramedics in.

"He's dead. I did it. Please just take me in sir and get me away from this house." I turned around willingly and waited for the first cop that stepped into the broken home I grew up in to place those cuffs on me and take me down to be processed. Just like that my life was over before I got a chance to really live and all for someone who didn't appreciate it. How dare she be mad at me?

3 months later.....

"I hereby sentence you Mr. Marque Johnson to the intense boot camp program. I sympathize with you sir for what you have gone through and I hope that with the aid of the program you are able to become a productive member of our society upon completion. I do not believe you intentionally meant to take a life. Good luck to you." With that the judge rose from his seat behind the bench and walked out the courtroom and I was on my way. I was relieved he considered this route rather than sending me to a detention hall or jail. My grandparents came through by getting me a great lawyer. They were so relieved to hear Mr.

Mack Johnson was no longer around to hurt their daughter however upset it was from my hands. My mother however had a hard time forgiving me. She is slowly coming around. She's receiving therapy and I guess it helps her see that the only one to blame is him. Another plus is now she has her parents back in her life. They moved to be by our side and she left the trailer.

I had my mind set up, I was going to complete this program and finish school then I want to enlist into the Army. I want to get out and see the world and protect my country and this would also be a way for me to give back. The judicial system could have smoked me but instead gave me a second chance.

CHAPTER ONE

Marque

After a long day at work, feeling relieved, I could finally clock out. It was a Saturday and as always, I had no work tomorrow. I came along way since being discharged from the Army. I'm a full-time employee for the United States Postal Service. It's how I am able to keep in shape, the amount of walking I do 6 days a week carrying mail in all kinds of weather here in Massachusetts. I decided to stop off at the grocery store and pick up something to eat and grab some flowers to bring with me to my girlfriend of the past 2 years house. I met Clover when I used to deliver mail in the area she lived in. It was freezing, and she opened the door to sign for a package offering me a thermos of the best tasting hot cocoa I have ever had. I had returned the thermos the following day to her and after time we started to engage in small talk until I asked her to dinner and she

9

accepted. Sounds like everything is perfect right, sadly that's far from the truth. You see we live in small town 70 miles west of Boston where not too many people share the same complexion as I do. Clover is fully Greek, and I am African American. Her family and friends have not approved of us and has sided with her ex-husband during a custody battle last week. He won physical custody of the kids, a 5-year-old son named Brock and a 3-year-old daughter named Baily. It didn't matter to anyone that I am a man with good credit, who served twice in the war in Afghanistan and I have a better job than her ex-husband. All they see is another black man with a criminal record, a man who killed his own father regardless of his reason and they feel that was a good enough reason to rip her children from her home. I tried to walk away from her for the sake of her children, but she wouldn't allow it, she was adamant she wasn't going to lose the best man to enter her life and she would fight til the end.

Walking in her door I found Clover wrapped up in a blanket holding a cup of what I can guess was tea with puffy eyes. I know she was crying. This was hurting me to the core seeing my girl so tore up over this. I put the flowers into a vase and went to start dinner. I chose to make chicken broccoli Alfredo with garlic bread. While the pasta was boiling, and the sauce was simmering I grabbed a water and joined Clover on the sofa. Instantly I could smell the liquor coming out her pores. I forgot to mention, she has turned to vodka and tries to hide it from me by drinking a cup of tea every night when I come by here. She knows how I feel about drinking outside of social events and I am starting to be concerned about her newfound habit. I hope it's only a phase due to the stress but if it's more than I am prepared to help her by supporting her and attend AA meetings.

"Did you eat today love?" I asked her.

She was so beautiful. With her stunning green eyes and dark brown hair that had natural waves but not what one would say is curly. She was thin but fit. However, the best feature she had that grabbed me from the start was her heart. I always got cold shoulders and nasty looks no matter how polite I was or how much I went above and beyond what my job description was but Clover right away was kind to me. She also didn't judge me when I told her one night about my past. I have severe nightmares, I wake up soaked in sweat at least once a week hollering. This is another reason we didn't live together. I don't want to keep someone awake when the episodes are more frequent than weekly. Besides taking my father's life, my second deployment overseas I seen my best friend killed in battle. But even with all I have gone through I still didn't turn to drugs or alcohol to help me cope.

I got up to check on the food and to start the shower. Another new routine for us. A shower before we actually eat. Me washing the days sweat off and her cleansing her pores of the alcohol she drank while I was at work. Turning the food down to simmer and letting Clover know that the water was ready she finally got up and walked towards her bathroom with me following her. I helped her undress and watched as she climbed inside. I then prepared to join her. Everything has become so systematic with us. It's as if I'm counting down in my head to the second on what will transpire next.

Bingo. Clover took a cloth and lathered it with soap. Starting from my neck and making her way down my body, all around to my chest and back. She cleaned me up head to toe. Finishing that she then dropped to her knees and took me into her mouth. Many men would love to be in this position right now and normally I would as well however like I just mentioned this has become a system. It's not fun when its expected. Few minutes into it I stopped her.

"Clover go ahead and wash up and meet me back in the kitchen okay." I didn't mean to sound so bored and cold but frankly that's just what I was. I cared about her beyond words could describe but something had to change soon, or I don't see a future much longer with us.

Stepping into her room which was across the hall from the bathroom I dried off and lotioned up. I put on some sweats and a beater, slid my feet in some slippers I left her room and headed to the kitchen to set the table. I am glad that I learned how to cook while in boot camp and the Army because the kitchen smelled so good right now.

Once Clover joined me we ate dinner and I must say tension was definitely in the air, so I decided to try and break it.

"Sorry for just leaving from the shower love. I'm just tired, sleep has been rough for me and I had extra work today. Old Mrs. Wilson got her hands-on Jacks card again and went crazy on buying stuff, so I had to double back to bring her a bunch of packages. I swear they need to be put into an assisted living program."

"Mmhmm." Was the only response I got, if she didn't feel like having a conversation then I wasn't going to force one on her. I dropped it and continued to eat dinner.

Finishing up I cleaned up the table and rinsed the dishes before placing them into the portable dishwasher I had surprised Clover with on Mother's Day last year and started a wash cycle. By the time I had finished she was in her room in bed and under her spread. Not really in the mood to stay and cuddle, I just grabbed a pair of socks, put on a tee, gave her a kiss on her forehead. I went in the other room to put my sneakers on, I was out of here.

Clover

I was laying in bed just staring up at my ceiling trying to figure out how can I get my life back. It is as if I have no control over myself most of the time and I am losing everyone behind it, but I refuse to lose anyone else; I can't lose Marque. Since the day I met him when I moved out of the home I shared with Robbie in Mendon I swore I was going to always have control of everything in my life because life with him was all but that. The day I met Marque when he rang the bell during the cold snowy day in January I was mesmerized by him. He had the perfect brown colored skin; his teeth were perfectly imperfect. His eyes told a story. Now here we are slowly falling apart, and I know it's my fault. I'm allowing the bottle to control my life. I know his feelings about consuming liquor he made it clear from the start yet every morning I wake up and drown myself in bottle after bottle until he comes over.

If only he could understand what it is like, growing up not thinking the same way your family and friends did yet pretended to just to fit in. Then having to marry someone you never loved because he worked at your uncle's garage and slipped you a date rape drug at a Christmas Party one year and you ended up pregnant. Having a family who believed your ex-husband over yourself each and every time he left bruises saying I provoked him. I really thought that once he finally went so far and I landed in the hospital needing surgery, had multiple broken ribs, not able to see out of either eye due to the blows he delivered to them, or the fact he had raped me over and over causing me to lose the baby they would finally believe me. But hey it was my fault, right? Wrong. I had to get out, so I took my kids, kids I wasn't ready for in life but loved nonetheless and moved out being cut off from everyone. Disowned and looked down upon for abandoning my husband and ripping the children away from him.

I remember the day me and Marque bumped into my auntie and cousins at the mall where we were school shopping for sneakers. Knowing the drama that was about to come because they seen Baily on Marque's shoulders and Brock holding my hand, it didn't matter to them that we all appeared happy and healthy. None of that got reported back to my parents. They even left out the bags I was carrying that I couldn't afford to shop at those named stores or that I didn't have to buy a single item, nor did I go to them for any help. All that mattered was I had my little girl sitting on top of a black man shoulders. I was still in the middle of a divorce and up until then not once did Ed even care to ask for sole and physical custody of our children so imagine the look on my face when we had court and I was told he was revising his request and was seeking such.

I miss my kids and I hope he is taking care of them and not putting his hands up to them when they cry or don't listen. He refused to take anything from my home to his saying they was infested with roaches he was just sure of. Funny part of it is, my house is clean while he is a slob.

I need to snap out of this funk. I need to do everything and make sure I keep my man and fight to get my children back, get my life back. I'm sure if I can prove that Ed isn't taking care of them correctly then I will have a chance. I had called over to the local child protective services putting in a private tip of abuse hoping when a worker showed up they would see the kids living in filth hungry and dirty but that backfired. It appears his new punching bag was on her job and the case went unfounded.

I got out of my bed, knowing Marque is long gone and more than likely asleep by now in his own bed, at the apartment he kept. I went into my stash cabinet which is in my son's room and grabbed a

14

bottle of Ruble Vodka, yes, the cheap stuff. I knew I was wrong to be hiding bottles in a child's room, but I didn't want Marque to discover them when cooking dinner as he has been doing for weeks. I walked back to my bedroom ready to have a lonely pity party of one when I remembered Marque never called nor texted me telling me he was home which is unlike him. Walking to my dresser I grabbed some panties and a tee, found some leggings and tossed them on. I grabbed my jacket, purse and keys and slipped into some Ugg's and went to drive by his house to make sure he had made it. Maybe I should have called first because I wasn't ready for what I seen.

CHAPTER TWO

Marque

I knew I wasn't going to be able to just go home and sleep. My mind was racing all over and all that awaited me at home was being alone and nightmares. It wasn't so much ending my father's life that haunted me as seeing my best friend be blown to pieces at a war where we had no place fighting. Nights such as tonight I would find myself visiting this little 24-hour café where I was just another late-night owl looking for a cup of coffee and some food.

Walking up to take a seat at the counter, the waitress Brenda smiled while carrying a coffee mug and a slice of apple pie. Placing the pie in front of me she proceeded to fix my coffee to perfection.

16

"Another rough night Marque?" Brenda placed the pot of coffee she used to fill my cup down on the counter and leaned her face into the palm of her hand.

"Same thing Brenda. Just tired and bored and what is better to ease one's mind than some good ole apple pie with a cup of coffee."

"Don't take offense Marque but when will you open up and let me in? It has been a few years now and I would like to consider you my friend. It was you who saw me through the hardest of times with your kind words and lending a shoulder even when I needed one to lean on."

"I have a girlfriend as you know, and it won't be fair to her if I turn to another woman when it should be her I am going to. It's complicated Brenda, because honestly, I feel like I can't even talk to her anymore. I feel like if I leave her while she is at a low point it would make me the monster her family painted me to be."

You see the thoughts have crossed my mind more than once about ending my relationship with Clover. I just felt stuck and somewhat responsible for her now that she lost everyone. I tried to use the custody situation as my way out, but she wasn't going for that and to be honest I wasn't expecting for a mother to choose a man before her children. Clover's idea of helping me and fixing my problems was always with intercourse. When I would have a nightmare, she would climb on top and we would have sex. If I had a bad day at work because someone new got the job promotion I was eyeing Clover would try to take my mind off of it in some sort of sexual way. It was great in the honeymoon part of the relationship but as I have stated I am just plain out bored with things.

"Well your girlfriend is just gonna have to understand that sometimes a person needs a different ear to vent to and I will be therapist Brenda in say about 30 minutes, so this pie and coffee is on the house while you wait Marque. Oh, and don't you leave and hide from me. Once this shift is over it's no longer waitress and customer chats it will be friends." With that Brenda turned around to place the coffee pot back in its place, started a fresh pot and began to stock up all the sugars and things to get everything ready for whoever was to take over.

For the first time in all the years I have stopped by here and interacted with Brenda I am looking at her in a whole new light. Bringing the cup to my lips to take a sip I was staring at her and I'm just amazed I never seen how perfect her smile was. The more I watched her getting ready to end her work day/night whichever one would prefer to call it the more I am coming to the conclusion that the coffee and pie weren't the only thing that has brought me here during my darkest moments but Brenda herself has. I loved seeing and interacting with this woman and it has taken me this very moment to admit it. I want this woman. I could feel the bulge growing in my sweats and just hope when it's time for me to stand and walk out the door it has calmed down. *Clover, Clover, Clover.* That is what I was saying over and over in my head. You are not that man Marque you have a girlfriend and guess what just like that my situation below had eased back down. It's pretty sad that when I look at another woman I get hard but when I think of my girlfriend of 2 years my erection goes away.

"You ready Suga? I texted my roomie and told her she didn't have to come scoop me and that I am sure you wouldn't mind dropping me off."

"It's the least I can do for my free pie right. Do you want to find a booth to sit in or what was your game plan seeing as this was your idea?" I asked her.

"Boy I am not about to hang around this place any longer than needed, I'm sure if they see me they will still look for me to help out.

18

We leaving from here but I really didn't have no destination in mind, but I am open to go anywhere."

"I guess my place is the answer unless you don't feel safe, but after all you demanded and being a gentleman, I am complying." I was secretly hoping she would agree to coming over for a little bit. Actually, I am praying she says yes because I would love to get to know Brenda outside of the diner and in her words not a waitress serving a customer but as a friend. How I never noticed before how attractive she was is crazy. She was a petite blonde, big doe shaped eyes with pouty lips.

"You're the driver so lead the way hun." And with that we were out the door and in my car heading towards my tiny one-bedroom apartment.

Stealing glances at Brenda as she danced in the seat singing along with every song that came on the radio, I decided to test her and switched to a different channel but that didn't matter because she fell in tune with what was playing.

"Music is my lifeline Marque. Whenever my parents would argue over me and my brother growing up I would just put my headphones on and listen to whatever was playing. Once I was old enough to sleep out I would always beg to spend the night over my best friend Gabby's. She and I went to school together. Her brother was a DJ/wedding singer so we would sit in the basement and watch him put together different lists for the upcoming events he was booked for. We would watch all the videos to learn all the dance moves that went with the song. Once we graduated High School I went away to college, however I never finished due to some craziness that took place."

Her voice dropped down after that and another weird feeling took over me. I was shocked to hear we both had a bad childhood.

You would never guess it by the bright personality she had along with positive energy that radiated from her. Stopping at a red light it was like I couldn't stop myself even if I wanted to. I leaned over and rubbed my hand gently down her face. I traced Brenda's lips with my finger and when she glanced up at me her eyes were sad, but her smile was ever so still amazing and showed strength and survival. Having zero self-control I kissed her, and it intensified. I completely forgot I was at a light until I heard the police siren.

They had pulled up on the side of me, so I looked over nodded and put my blinker on, so I could pull over when he yelled across the cars bullhorn

"PUT YOUR HANDS UP, DO NOT MOVE. I REPEAT DO NOT MOVE. DRIVER LET ME SEE YOUR GOD DAMN HANDS! NOW MOTHERFUCKER. DON'T GIVE ME A REASON TO USE MY WEAPON!"

Doing just as I was ordered I asked Brenda to put my car into park while my foot was still on the break. I didn't want to give this officer any reason to follow through with the threat he just made. I understood it loud and clear.

He walked up to my car and opened my door with his government assigned Glock 22 handgun, aimed right at my head. I was thinking all this occurred because I didn't move right away when the light turned green. It was a little extreme in my opinion but I wasn't going to voice such, not while he was clearly an unstable white officer with a gun aimed at a black man's head.

"Get out the car slowly, walk towards the back and place your hands on the trunk." Doing as I was told, not putting up a fight, he grabbed both my hands and shoved me toward the trunk of my car, never given me the chance to walk myself. Once he placed cuffs, extremely tight I may add, he patted me down.

"May I ask what is this for sir. I was about to pull over. I do.."

"Shut the hell up! Did I ask you to speak? Just get down on the ground and speak when I tell you to, do you hear me boy?"

"Yes sir." I was angry, but I have seen so many videos lately of life's being taken in situations just like the one I was currently in. So, I just went with it.

He proceeded to my car, opened my back door and appeared to be searching around. Good luck because all he would see is my uniform and a gym bag. I just smiled because I know he was about to be mad as hell. He just mistreated me when he simply could have said pay attention to the lights, but he assumed because I am a black man with a nice car I was doing wrong.

"Whose vehicle is this boy?" he asked looking over at me as he stood with the door still open, holding up my work uniform with an expression that clearly showed he was surprised I also worked for the government.

"Mine officer." I stated.

"Do you know this man?" I heard him asking Brenda and this is where I got pissed the hell off. Of course, she knew me, she was in my car and he clearly seen me kissing her but at least she will be able to verify that I am indeed the owner of the car and the uniform seeing as he found it hard to believe that a young black man had a legal good paying job in this part of the state. All he had to do was ask for some identification but the more I thought about it, I'm relieved he didn't because me reaching for my wallet could be a reason for him to shoot my ass and the law would justify it just as they do every other police involved killing of innocent people.

"Yes officer, he is my friend Marque who was so kind to

come out this late and pick me up from work due to my roommate feeling under the weather. Is there a problem?" I could hear the anger mixed with sarcasm in Brenda's voice, something tells me this ain't her first encounter with this specific cop. Which I kind of was hoping was the case, because her being sarcastic won't help me any.

"Cut the bullshit Brenda. I know Melanie is just fine, I was just by the house so why are you really getting a ride which by the way clearly wasn't heading towards the house." Now I am confused. Brenda knows this cop, and this was not a random stop, but he was following us from her job looking for a reason to pull me over. I knew the patrol cars had cameras, so he was going to need something to back up his claim. Could he be an ex of her?

"Rob shut up and let Marque get up from the ground. You're so annoying I swear. Let us go. I am no longer your little sister who you scare" Brenda got out the car removed his keys from his belt loop and uncuffed me.

"Let's go Marque. I didn't realize it was my asshole brother at first."

This should have been my warning to just say hey bro take your sister home will ya and I carried my black ass on home, but I didn't want to give him the satisfaction I'm sure he was looking for. It felt good for just a split second to semi have the upper hand.

"Come on Brenda, let me get you home. Maybe we can talk another time. It's been a long enough night." I didn't even look at her. I was mad. My blood was boiling. I'm tired of being judged by the color of my skin. Treated like I am beneath others. I got in my car, slamming the door surprising myself that it didn't shatter. I buckled up, beeped the horn so she could get in so we could be on our way.

22

"Marque please don't do this. I like you okay. I have for a long time now. That kiss you just gave me was everything. Don't allow the hate my brother has ruin tonight. Can I please still come over and talk. I need someone just like you do, someone who has a past filled with hurt and guilt. I am scared to allow someone fully in, so maybe we can help heal each other fully. Let me be that person for you, I want you to be that person for me. You can't deny it, I see it when our eyes meet so stop fighting it."

She was right. Until this evening when I was frustrated, and she was walking towards me with my usual order did I realize that I was just going through the phases of life with Clover; playing a role I was assigned to do. I didn't love her, and I definitely wasn't living a happy life with her.

Not looking to give another cop a reason to pull my black ass over, I put my left blinker on and eased back onto the road slowly. I grabbed her hand, squeezed it and carried on to my apartment. I don't even think I wanted to talk anymore tonight. At this point I just wanted to lay down and hold her. I can wait for another opportunity to arise to learn her story and tell her mine.

Clover

My eyes can't be deceiving me, could they? Was I really seeing the man I gave so much up for, the man I loved more than anything or anyone else laying in his bed with another woman wrapped in his arms, head on his chest while he was playing in her hair. He looked to be deep in thought and she was so comfortable. I wonder how long this has been going on for? Was I that out of it that I couldn't see the signs that my man was living a different life? I refuse to sit back and allow this to happen. He is mine and after all I sacrificed for him he was going to remain mine.

Choosing to not let it be known that I discovered his secret I turned around got in my car and headed home. I needed to think and think fast on how I was going to get this woman out the way and show Marque that I was it for him. I also know enough to know that it wouldn't be easy for him to replace her, so I needed to do more than just have her disappear.

I walked in the door, not bothering to lock it and headed right for my stash. I had dropped the bottle I had took with me when I seen Marque and his lover together outside his bedroom window. Opening the closet, a thought came to my mind. He hates the fact I drink so maybe if I stop and deal with things better he will remember why he chose me to begin with. Yes, that's it. I will get rid of the bottles, so one by one I walked and dumped everything out and emptied the trash. I then put some music on not caring what time of night it was. I was on a mission. I cleaned the whole house. Washed all curtains and dusted. Sleep began to hit me, so I took another shower and laid down. Telling myself only a few hours nap then I wanted to get up to fix up my appearance.

Well those few hours turned into many. I woke up seeing it was night. My stomach was grumbling and felt nauseous. I rolled over and couldn't believe it was 9pm. Grabbing my phone, I seen I had no missed calls or texts from Marque which instantly made me mad. Then I could hear the shower running and I noticed his bag on the floor by my bedroom door. I got up and walked into the kitchen and seen he had brought some take out, maybe that was what woke me and what made my stomach feel queasy. Not being able to fight it anymore I ran for the bathroom and just as I opened the door and leaned over the toilet Marque was getting out of the shower. Looking at me with a frown on his face and not a bit of concern for what was going on with me at that moment, he just walked into my room leaving me alone praying to the porcelain gods to help me.

I finally was able to get up, so I cleaned up the toilet washed out my mouth and walked to my room. Marque was sitting on the edge of my bed and it seemed like he had a heavy load on his mind. I took a seat next to him and tried to lay my head on his shoulder, but he brushed me off.

"Clover I think you need help. I tried to stay out of it and let you get it out of your system but look at you. Sleeping all day, barely eating and drinking all damn day. Do you see all the fucking bottles in that trash can outside? You are lucky to be alive and not in a hospital suffering from alcohol poison. You drank more than a frat house filled with men last night. I can't continue to do this. I'm sorry Clover I am." He kissed me on the forehead and grabbed not just the usual bag but a few bags that he must have packed while I was getting sick in the bathroom and walked out. He didn't just walk out the room, but out my life.

I just broke down. This can't be. He didn't even let me speak or explain that I was going to get help, that last night I decided to come clean and stop drinking because I love him so much. Not being able to help myself I jumped up and went to follow him. I needed to see where he was going, was he going right home, or would he be running to the woman he was secretly messing with.

Seeing him just sit outside of a diner while the same woman appeared to be saying bye to her co-workers had me going back over the many many nights he left the house at certain times; was this the real reason? So, he could pick his lover up? I watched him get out the car and give her a hug and kiss and help her into his car and then they proceeded to his house. Parking a little way up yet close enough I was able to see into his apartment, I could see them laughing at what was on his tv while he fed her popcorn. I can't remember when was the last time I seen him so happy. How was I so blind? I got out my car and found a brick and smashed his window. When the alarm went off he came running out the building and seen me standing there with tears falling. His expression didn't show any sign that he was sorry that he had broke my heart, he showed zero sympathy for the fact I was frozen crying.

"Are you crazy Clover? What are you even doing here.? And why are you standing in nothing?"

I was so mad I forgot to even get dressed and up until he said something I didn't even realize it.

"Is everything okay baby?" ugh could her voice be any more annoying I thought.

"I have everything under control love, go back inside I will be right in."

He just blatantly disrespected me! Wow I can't believe this shit! Who was this man and where did he put the man who was always so attentive and loving?

"No everything is not ok you home wrecking whore. You're fucking my man and coming between my family. I'm pregnant Marque you asshole and this is the thanks I get. I fucking hate you and I promise you will pay. But don't worry keep your Barbie because I'll be making an appointment to have this bastard child sucked out of me. It's better off before it comes out to be damaged like your murderous ass. You killed your father, you killed me, you kill everything that comes in contact with you. You couldn't even save your best friend, you stood and watched him blow up." I really didn't mean all of what I said but I wanted him to feel the pain that he had caused me.

I took off running and jumped in my car and sped off. A few minutes passed, and I seen that Marque was calling my phone back to back, but I was ignoring him. I don't even know what possessed me to say I was pregnant. But I guess he believed me and the fact two hours earlier he seen me bent over the toilet bowl helped support my story. According to the voice messages and the texts he wanted to talk with me about what I just dropped on him.

This was not the end and it was not over. I promise.

CHAPTER THREE

Marque

Things with Brenda has been nothing short of amazing. Her family was loving and accepting. We both opened up to our fears and past traumas. I learned that she had started to date another black male she had met when she was away at college. I also learned that he had went to jail for being in possession of a large quality of cocaine along with some firearms, which he swore was a set up. She tried to stand by his side, but he shut her out, blaming her and her brother for being in his current position. I guess brother dearest has a problem with his sister dating outside her race and for that reason he was no longer close to anyone in his family. His parents didn't condone his behavior. His girlfriend had even ended it with him. I found out I wasn't the first man he tried to use his badge to scare off and what he did placed no fear at all in me, well outside of the fact

28

that if he found a way he could set me up or worse kill me and use his badge for a defense. Maybe if Brenda wasn't still in the car that night maybe he would have planted something in it but thankfully that didn't happen. My nightmares have eased a lot and for the first time in all my life everything was how life should be, well almost everything. I guess Brenda losing her ex behind her brother was what was troubling her. She felt she couldn't live and love and be happy as long as he wore the badge he did.

Clover has become a major issue. She swears she is pregnant and goes from hot to cold. She tried to have me fired from my job. She will text me she got an abortion and call me everything, but the child of god yet turns around and leaves me messages how she is going to take her life and our unborn if I don't talk to her. Brenda has encouraged me to seek an order of protection, but I don't think it's needed. Maybe by me ignoring her and the possibility she is being truthful about having my baby is wrong, but I am afraid that if she is indeed having my child then what I have with Brenda could suffer. Just by how Clover is acting I know she will make my life with anyone other than her hell. How could I not have seen this side of her prior? What made her just snap like this. I do care for her, but I just don't love her. I wish she could understand that. She was the one who changed and pushed me into the arms of another woman. I wanted Clover to take a test and bring me proof that she was with child, but she never would come through with the documentation.

I had got a phone call from my grandparents that my mother was not doing well. She went to the doctors and found out she had stage 4 breast cancer and was getting weaker by the day and she keeps asking for me to stop by and see her. Today is that day and I am bringing Brenda with me. Oh, what I left out is my mother wanted to die in her home, so she had moved back to the hellhole I grew up in. I knew I was going to need all the support I could find, and Brenda understood. Driving along but this time as a passenger my mind was all over the place. I began searching for one good memory growing up in that home and kept coming up blank.

Brenda had suggested that I go speak with someone and get prescribed something before heading out, but I felt like I didn't need it. I could handle it, I was sure of it.

The closer she got the worse I began to feel. I was getting clammy. I started to see that bastards face everywhere. Maybe this wasn't a good idea, but it is too late now. We drove 3 hours to get here and I will just go in and spend a little bit of time then leave out. Pulling into the trailer park it looked worse than I pictured. I have never looked back since the night I was arrested. I tried to muster up the strength to get out and greet my grandparents who was standing outside awaiting my arrival.

Brenda put the car in park, turned the engine off, took her seatbelt off and turned her body facing me.

"Marque baby. I know walking in that door is going to be hard, but you're not alone. I will be right next to you the whole time. Try to focus on the purpose of being here only and that is to spend some time with your mother because her days are numbered." She was speaking softly, and I felt each word she said.

"I don't understand why she would want to come here of all places to die baby? Life was hell here, she never smiled. I heard her cry more than laugh. I have no regrets and I swear I would do it all over again."

"It's not for us to understand why she chose here, only your mother knows the reason behind that. Come on love. Sitting here in the car isn't going to make it go away."

She was right yet again. I swear I was blessed to have a woman like her in my life. Once we make it back home I am going to go by Clovers and get that situation taken care of. In the short time I have been with Brenda, ain't no doubt she was put on this earth to be with me and I plan on spending forever with her. She was my peace, my sanity, my heart and soul.

Embracing my grandparents and slowly stepping inside the broken trailer the smell was horrible. I turned to walk out but Brenda just put her hand in mine and gave me a look. Taking a deep breathe I walked towards the beeping machines that hospice had hooked up to my mother. They had made a makeshift hospital room out of the living area. Sitting down next to her I looked, and the tears instantly fell. This shell of a woman wasn't my mother. They looked nothing alike. My mother was always a fragile woman but who laid in the bed before me looked to be a corpse already. She had a scarf tied around her head, her eyes was sunken in. She must have sensed me because she then opened them, barely I must add.

Smiling looked like it hurt her but nonetheless she smiled as big as she could.

"My beautiful baby boy. You came. Thank you. I know this is the last place you ever wanted to be, but I choose here to die because of you. Not him. I wanted to be where my best memories took place Marque. It was here you took your first steps. Where I heard the words, I love you mama for the first time. I am so sorry Marque I failed you. It has taken this disease for me to see the wrong and damage I have caused you as a child by staying all those years with him because of the love I thought was real. Truth is ain't no real love than a mother's love for her child. One day you will be a parent and you will understand more than I could. Please my boy forgive me, I am so sorry Marque. I love you." She began to cough and cry and couldn't seem to stop. The machines were going crazy and the nurses asked us to step out. I didn't want to I had to tell my mother

31

before it was too late, and I needed her to hear something.

"Ma I forgive you for everything and it's me who is sorry for not ending it sooner, so you could find happiness. I want you to meet someone. Brenda come here please. Ma this is Brenda and she completes me, she makes me so happy. I find comfort in a simple touch of hers and before you take your last breath I want to do this."

I turned towards Brenda and got on one knee

"I know we are fresh, but I mean all I said to my mother. I love you and you're the greatest thing to have happened in my life. I want to walk out this door and not have a haunted memory but create a beautiful new memory in a place I feared the most. Brenda will you please accept my hand in marriage and be my wife?"

"YES" she screamed, as tears fell from her eyes. I placed the ring on her finger and turned back towards my mother.

"I like her Marque and I know you will be a great husband and father. Take care of my boy Brenda." And with that my mother took her last breath.

My mama may have taken her last breath, but I think we was all holding ours. I was speechless. I felt like a huge weight lifted off me however I am filled with regret. Regret I didn't take more time to talk to my mother. I am relieved however that she choose here not so that she died in the home that asshole did but because of the memories she held onto of me as a child.

I was ready to go. Wiping the few tears that fell I said my goodbyes to my grandparents and told them to call me when they wanted to make arrangements. Brenda gave my nana a hug and kiss on the cheek and made plans to get together soon for tea. Tea, do you believe that? Who does those things anymore, but I guess she wanted to make a better impression on my grandmother.

The drive home was peaceful. No words were spoken because they weren't needed. Today will be the first day of the beginning of a great new life. I do know that we have to address the situation with Clover.

Clover

Seeing the obituary for the bitch of a mother that had Marque then flipping the page and seeing the engagement announcement for Brenda and him printed on the same day really blew my mind. I understand he hated that lady in his own way but to celebrate her death by asking a stranger for her hand in marriage when here I am carrying his child is crazy. I mean okay, so I never got a test done but I swear I see the bump growing and I can't smell many things wit hout getting sick. I went back to drinking. Why not, I mean the bottle didn't give up on me or desert me. No-one came along and ripped a bottle from my life like my kids and Marque was.

Hearing a car pull up to the driveway I didn't bother to move, for what. I'm sure it was just the city to leave another warning on my door about me not taking the trash out or maybe it was to threaten to shut the water off. Either way I ain't interested in what they wanted.

"Open the door Clover, I know you are home." I heard Marque say.

Oh my god could it be true, maybe he woke up and realized what he was doing was wrong and he was here to say sorry and let's be a family.

I jumped up running to the door but the look on his face wasn't one of lust.

"Clover why do you have all these tickets and warnings on your door. Come on girl. This is why I had to walk away. If you are pregnant you had to have caused damage to our baby by now with the liquor."

He stepped inside then right back out.

"Matter of fact go shower put something on and let's go, I can't stand the stench inside your house and I refuse to have this overdue conversation with you here."

In my head all I heard was go get dressed baby I'm here to take you and the baby out of here, so we can be happy, so naturally I did as I was told. Pulling up to a parking lot not of somewhere to eat or even some where people go on a date Marque shut his car off and told me to come on.

Walking next to him I tried to grab his hand, but he moved his before I could clasp his fingers. Confused I had to ask "Why are you so cold to me Marque? Baby aren't you happy we going to be a family soon, you came back."

Stopping in place he looked down then back at me taking a deep breath and sighing.

"That is the furthest thing from my mind. I went to your house to talk about everything and say sorry for my part in walking away. I told you from the beginning how I felt about drinking and I tried to understand you was using it to cope with all that went down with Brock and Baily, but I stopped loving you. Actually, you stopped loving yourself. We were stuck and felt obligated to stay together to prove to your family that what we had was real but in reality, at least I was lying. I didn't know it at first but as time passed my love just stopped growing."

"SHUT UP MARQUE!" I yelled, and I noticed some other

34

people parked some ways down looked our direction

"That's a lie and you know it, she is drugging you ain't she. We are having a baby, here feel my stomach." He actually did look down, but he had a puzzled look on his face.

"Clover is everything okay? We never discussed mental illness, but I don't know why you think your pregnant, your stomach is actually smaller than it was months ago."

Was he really questioning my mental status? Had he came home every night and been a man and rubbed my back like most fathers do when expecting a child while I was emptying the contents of my stomach then he would see what I know to be true.

Just then it hit me, I'm not pregnant, I had my tubes fixed after Baily because I didn't want any more children. If I wasn't pregnant than what was making me so sick and what could I use to keep Marque in my life. Clearly, he moved on and was happy with that Brenda girl. Brenda? Ha! What kind of life could she give him? She served coffee for God's sake! Then again, she did more than I did so I guess that is just another plus she has on me.

Letting out a scream I lost it

"STOP IT MARQUE, LEAVE ME ALONE. WHY ARE YOU DOING THIS TO ME. STOP IT STOP HURTING ME." As I began to hit myself over and over in the face pulling my hair.

"SOMEONE HELP ME PLEASE HELP ME, CALL THE POLICE CALL AN AMBULANCE HE IS HURTING ME AND MY UNBORN BABY!"

CHAPTER FOUR

Marque

"What are you doing Clover? Stop hitting yourself. Come on let me take you to the hospital for an evaluation. This is not what I want for you. I still care about you and think about your kids."

I tried to reach for her to help her into the car because it don't take someone with 20/20 vision to see she needed to be put into a mental hospital. She is having a real life mental breakdown out here in public and one thing I won't do is fail her as a friend. Before I could even get my arms around her I felt something hard come down on my head.

"Don't you fucking move bitch. You want to put your hands on a white woman huh well not on my watch."

Rolling over to my back I looked up and go figure out of all the cops that could have came it had to be this asshole who had it out for me because I was with his sister.

"Listen I didn't do anything, I am trying to help her. She needs medical attention." I was trying to reason with him hoping he would just hear me out.

"You lying piece of dirt, look at her she has the marks and backup is on the way, blink your mother fucking eye the wrong way or twitch and it will be lights out for you."

Yeah, he definitely is one of these badge abusing power control assholes. I just hope that a witness comes forward and soon to tell them that I didn't touch her at all. Better yet she needs to snap out of it and tell the damn truth. I understand she is hurt but I didn't deserve this.

"Bro please listen to me, call Brenda she can vouch for me, I came to talk to this woman. She is my ex. She has been stalking me and your sister and I just wanted to peacefully resolve it. She flipped out I didn't touch her. Call your sister, ask a witness." I was pleading, and it made me sick that I had to kiss a mother fuckers' ass when I did no wrong.

"It is you, you know I wasn't so sure at first because you know you look like every other woman beating black boy. Oh, I can't wait to rub this shit here in my sister's face. Another fucking loser she found. Just like that music kid. Thought he could take her innocence and walk free, nope I fixed his ass."

This can't be my reality right now. I began to pray, and I mean pray hard that someone with reason and some sense showed up because right now all I could see was a deranged ex and a cop with a grudge and both was not on my side.

Well I guess he didn't like my silence too much because he began attacking me, swinging that billy stick all over my body and yelling stop resisting when clearly, I wasn't. I just hope someone had a camera going, that is one good thing that has gone in victims of police brutality these days. Was always someone with a phone in their hand trying to capture the next viral video instead of doing the right thing and speaking up or even helping.

It felt like the assault was never ending and finally I couldn't take it no more. I had to protect myself, or he was going to kill me with that long black stick. I kicked my leg up catching him right in his little ole dick. Time was not on my side because it was that moment that his backup arrived and I felt something hot burn right through my chest. I could feel myself slipping but I managed to look at Rob and said, "I hope you rot in hell. I know Brenda won't rest until you pay you bitch." With that, I closed my eyes.

Brenda

Marque has been gone for over 5 hours and I was beginning to worry. Not so much that he had ran off and decided he was going to go back with Clover, but I had this horrible feeling in the pit of my stomach that she might have hurt him some way. I tried to tell him to get a stay away order against her, that she was crazy, but he told me she was harmless. That night she showed up at his place and smashed the window wasn't the only time she had stalked us. I would see her all the time parked in the parking lot of the diner just watching me work. I may not like my brother, nor speak to Rob but I was glad that when he knew I was at work late nights he made sure to patrol the area, so her insane ass couldn't do anything to me.

I decided to go take a hot bubble bath and try to calm my nerves a little bit and wait for Marque to call me. Melanie, my roommate and best friend was in the living room watching the news and talking on the phone to one of her friends when I heard her scream my name. I climbed out the tub and slid my bathrobe on to see what was wrong. She was standing in front of the T.V. with a look of shock plastered on her face.

"What's wrong?" I asked her still clueless.

"Sit down Brenda." She said with the remote to the T.V. on pause.

"Tell me what is wrong, you have me scared."

"It's Marque." She started to say but I didn't hear the rest, my legs had given out from under my body and I fell on the floor. I didn't know what was wrong exactly with him, but I know I been feeling something had happened to him.

"Brenda, can you hear me?" Melanie was in front of me trying to lift me from the floor.

I jumped up and said, "Bring me to that hoe's house, I'm going to show her crazy for hurting my fiancé."

"It wasn't her who hurt him, they said it was a police officer involved incident and your brother was on the scene." She informed me.

"He better not have been the one that did this to Marque, oh my god Marque! You never told me what happened. Is he…" my voice trailed off and I was unable to utter my greatest fear out my mouth.

"The news just said he is in critical condition. So, go hurry and put clothes on so we can go up the hospital." Melanie said.

Arriving at the hospital about an hour later because he was transferred to Mass General, I noticed the media vans parked outside with newscasters hanging around. I guess for an updated report on Marque's condition to report on the next airing. Thankfully we were just average people and not celebrities, so I was able to walk inside without being bombarded with questions. Right now, I just wanted to get to whatever section they had him in and find out from medical personnel how he was and what was his chances of survival. On my way here, Rob had tried to call me numerous times, but I didn't want to hear anything from him, I am sure it wouldn't be accurate no way.

"Hello, I'm here to see my fiancé Marque Johnson." I said to the next available front desk agent. Mass General is one of the top hospitals in the country, so they needed just as many receptionists as a major bank did when the first and third of the month needed when they fell on a payday mixed with tax season. It was always busy.

"Do you have any identification, we will need to call security before we can give you a visitor pass and if your friend is trying to visit I will need her ID as well." The white haired elderly woman inquired while nodding her head towards Melanie.

"I do." I stated while looking in my purse for it and handing it off as Melanie did the same. This was insane if you asked me, I was trying to see a patient in the hospital not an inmate at a correctional facility. However, I wasn't going to make a big deal out of it because I didn't want to risk anything from not being granted access. Seeing as she was now on the phone giving my name to who I assumed was someone in security.

"Very well sir." She said as she hung up the phone and was pressing keys on the desktop computer in front of her and printed out two visitor passes handing them to us along with our ID's and gave us instructions on how to get to the ICU.

Approaching the double doors with Intensive Care Unit in bold black letters written above it, I heard my name being called from a room just on the side of it. I looked over and seen Marque's grandmother. I walked into the room and introduced Melanie to his grandparents and took a seat.

"Have they told you how he is or what exactly is wrong with him?" I had asked his grandfather because his grandmother was talking to Melanie.

"They said the first 24 hours are going to be the worst. If he makes it past that then they believe he will be okay." He replied.

"What about the police? Have they talked to you and told you what took place? I had a bad feeling all afternoon and had just got in the bath when my roommate yelled for me because she seen something on the news." I had asked no one in particular.

"No, they sent an officer to the house and informed us that he was in a parking lot with that hussy Clover when an altercation took place, a passerby had called the cops and he had got into it with the officer that had showed up, while fighting with that officer another had showed up and said it looked like he was reaching for the cops gun so he shot him." His grandmother had filled me in.

"Will you excuse me while I step out in the hall to make a phone call?' Melanie said, and I knew she was about to go off on my brother. We both suspected he had his hand in this. On our way to Boston we were discussing if it was possible but hearing that he was fighting with a cop basically confirmed it for me that it was my brother. I was in the car the night he pulled Marque over and he followed orders, so I don't see why he wouldn't cooperate this time.

"Do you think I can go in the back and sit with him for a few minutes?"

"Of course, you can hunny, Marque needs all the love and support and I'm sure in his mind he is waiting on hearing your voice." His grandmother said.

I just nodded my head and went to pick up the phone on the wall to let the nurses know I was here to see him and be buzzed in.

CHAPTER FIVE

Marque

I could hear the beeping of machines, but I wasn't able to open my eyes. I tried to pay attention to the voices in the distance talking, but I didn't recognize any of them. They were discussing my chances of waking up and how it would be up to me to wake up. I know my grandparents are here somewhere, I could hear my grandmother sobbing over me and my grandfather consoling her, reassuring her that it wasn't my time and it's just a minor setback.

When I tell you, I smelled her scent before I heard her voice, it soothed me. I want to wake up so bad and say sorry for not taking her advice and doing something about Clover sooner.

"Baby, your grandmother told me to just come in and let you know that I'm here and I'm not leaving until you wake up. We have a future to spend together, a wedding to plan. I never told you this, but I want 3 kids, 2 boys and 1 girl maybe even a dog to chase them around the yard, but I don't just want this with anyone. I need you to wake up, I need for you to tell me what happened and why was you in a parking lot and not at Clover's getting to the bottom of her saying she was pregnant. More importantly, I need for you to confirm what my heart is already telling me and did Rob do this to you?"

When she said that I felt my heart start to race. I was angry and had every right to be. I was shot because I was defending myself from her brother. I love this woman, but maybe I should break things off with her if I wake up. I don't want to look over my shoulder for the rest of my life because her brother has a problem with her dating a black man. I know it's not fair to her, listening to her visions of our little perfect family, but as long as she was with me, that dream won't happen if her brother has anything to do with it. I already know that he will get away with the assault he placed on me and his colleague will get away with putting a bullet in me. It's just the cold reality of how the law worked.

Unlike the vow I took when I enlisted in the Armed Forces, most police officers didn't believe or didn't care to understand the meaning behind, To Protect & Serve. Most of them were bullied as kids and used the badge for a power trip, to be able to assault and harass innocent people because they had the authority to do so. I took honor in the vow I made to protect the country in which I was a proud citizen of and swore by my commitment. However, here I lay in a bed, not able to open my eyes or communicate with anyone because I am a black man in America dating a white woman whose is a victim of police brutality.

Brenda stayed by my bedside for about an hour just talking to me, then I would hear her started sobbing softly as if she didn't want me to hear her keep breaking down. Eventually she stood up, kissed me on the forehead, and told me she had something she had to take care of and would be back the next day. The tone in her voice was off and kind of alarming.

Although I knew that when I pulled through this situation, I was going to walk away from a beautiful soul. I wished she was still sitting by my bedside because at least someone was talking to me and I wasn't just listening to an occasional gossip conversation between the nurses outside my room or the beeping of machines. Then when they would call code blue for someone the room next to me. I don't know what was wrong with that person but they sure was a fighter, because in the few hours I was moved to this unit, code blue has been called 3 times. I said a silent prayer for the person and tried to rest my own mind. I was going crazy not being able to wake up and communicate. I don't understand, if they say that an individual in a coma can hear you speak to them, why wouldn't they put a T.V. or something in the room? I would die, no cross that, I'd do anything right now even to listen to the news; shit infomercials sounds good at this point. Anything is better than the noise in my room and the thoughts in my head. Normally when it's quiet like it is now, this is when I get flashbacks to my second deployment and seeing Ethan blown to pieces right before my eyes. Had I not stopped to readjust the heavy bag filled with gear that I was carrying, I very well could have been close enough where I would have blown up with him. Sometimes, I wish I did.

Ethan became my closest friend right from the jump. He came from a good family, filled with high ranking Army vets. Prior to being deployed the second time, we actually became roommates and lived closer to his family. He grew up closer to the city, where diversity wasn't bad, so we agreed that once that first mission was completed, and we returned to the states that it only made sense to live by his family in the city of Revere Massachusetts.

Outside of the short time in my relationship with Brenda, maybe even the early days with Clover, living in Revere with Ethan was the happiest times of my life. To be welcomed in to his family with open arms and shown what a normal family life was all about didn't bring me down because I had such a shitty childhood, but he gave me hopes and dreams of having my own family one day and doing all that I could to see that we were just as close as Ethan's. We were only living in our 2- bedroom 2 bath condo right on Revere Beach for 6 months before we were notified of another deployment we had to leave for.

Ironically, I had dreams of signing up for the police academy and using my resume from the Army to help me get in. As I mentioned, Ethan comes from a family of high ranking veterans, many who once they returned from overseas, they became some form of a first responder. They assured me that they would be able to assist me in being accepted in the academy even though I had that conviction of murder on my C.O.R.I. which is a criminal offender record information system. It is a program many jobs along with landlords use to check for any past criminal activity.

All that changed once I lost Ethan to a bomb on the side of a dirt road. I was still deployed and couldn't attend the services. When I finally was able to return back to America, I never responded to the numerous attempts his family had made for me to come visit. I never returned to our condo to pick up any of my belongings. I had hoped that they would have shipped the stuff to my grandparent's home, but they never did. I missed Ethan. Maybe when I wake up I will reach out to his family, find out where he is buried, and go sit and talk with the only male friend I ever had.

"Cold Blue, Code Blue" came across the loudspeakers of the hospital yet again and I could hear the commotion outside my room but this time after a few minutes I heard them call the patients time of death and heard the attending doctor say he will call the family to notify them. I said a prayer for that person along with his family.

Clover

I didn't want all that took place in that parking lot to happen. I never suspected that Marque would be shot. I just wanted him to be in jail for a little bit and get him away from that bitch that stole him from me. I know if he wasn't under her spell that he would recall why he was with me originally. When I heard that gun go off and seeing Marque fall, his fresh white shirt turning red from the blood that was oozing out of the wound on his chest, I lost it

"What the fuck did you do? Why did you shoot him?" I screamed while trying to get to Marque and tell him I loved him, and I will be right up the hospital.

"He was reaching for his gun. I heard my brother say don't touch my gun!" the officer that shot Marque had said.

"Brother, y'all don't look alike." I pointed out with a confused look on my face. One of the cops was tall very thin and had a face only a mother would love; the other one who was the first on the scene was average height, very nice build where you could tell he took care of his body and was extremely handsome.

"Ma'am not brother in the family aspect but brother as in the police force." The officer who originally was fighting with Marque said to me.

One of the bystanders yelled out that Marque was not to blame, and I wasn't assaulted. I shot daggers in his direction for trying to lie on me. Okay maybe it wasn't fully a lie, but Marque had hurt me by walking away from our relationship and for another woman. However, with all the commotion none of the officers paid any attention to the bystander to even take a statement.

I don't want Marque to die but I don't regret the assault I put on myself and yelling for help which led to all that is going on in front of me.

"Ma'am, we are going to need for you to come down to the station after being seen at the hospital for the marks."

"Go to the station for what? I am a victim of domestic violence and I didn't pull no trigger so what do you need from me?"

"Relax, we just need a statement from you on the events that took place today. It is strictly procedure. We are sure that the press has already gotten wind of this and we need to cross all of our T's and dot our I's with this investigation." He informed me then he added, "An ambulance is en route to take you as well as Mr. Johnson to the hospital to be seen."

"Can't I just ride with him? I never wanted for him to get hurt." I asked.

"I'm afraid you can't. The local hospital is not equipped to handle the severity of his injuries, so he will be transported to Mass General in Boston. I'm sure he will be okay. I heard he was responsive and is fading in and out of consciousness."

"Okay but why can't I ride with him still and be seen at the same hospital?" I asked puzzled.

"Ma'am for one, your injuries are not sufficient enough, two, the EMT's will need the room in the back to treat Mr. Johnson en route to the hospital so no one is allowed to ride even in the front." He told me now looking at me with a fucked-up expression.

"Oh, but my injuries are severe enough, I'm pregnant and I'm having severe cramping."

"We have a birthing unit at the local hospital that can tend to your needs."

I had to think quick. I wanted to go to the same hospital as Marque. I had to be able to check on him. Looking around I noticed that the light at the intersection was about to turn green, so I ran off and jumped in front of the car that was trying to make a go for it and get from having to be at a red light, so it picked up its speed. I felt an excruciating pain shoot up from my leg instantly then when I landed my head smacked off the ground and everything turned black.

CHAPTER SIX

Marque

Tick tock, tick tock. This is really starting to bother me. I'm bored and really want to wake up and move on with my life. It's been 3 days now, and although I am grateful at times that I survived I would much rather be doing something than lay here with my thoughts. My grandparents have been up here every day for a few hours, and Brenda basically moved in here. She sits by my bed and just talks, tells me stories about her childhood. Her dreams, her plans for us. I had every intention of walking away from her once I came too, but the news she is telling me right now makes it impossible.

"So yeah, that is where I have been for the past two hours, downstairs in the emergency room. The test came back positive, so we need for you to wake up now okay. We want you to be at the first official appointment with the Dr." she said with joy in her voice.

I haven't heard this tone since I have been laying here.

"I'm clearly not showing or anything but here feel the home your first born will be residing for the next few months." Brenda said while picking my hand up and placing it on what I knew was her stomach.

I have to stay, I have to be a man, I always vowed not to be who my father was and to treat the mother of my child with respect and love and honor her. I won't break her heart, I won't hurt her, I won't do any of what that man did to my mother. As she was pulling her hand away from her stomach, I wasn't ready to stop feeling it so I pulled my hand away from hers thinking it was just in my mind that I did that until I heard her scream out for someone to come in my room.

"He pulled his hand from mine! What's that mean, it's good right?" she beamed with excitement in her voice.

"Could be, or it could have been just the muscles naturally reacting. If you will step out the room and give us a chance to look at Mr. Johnson, we will have more information to tell you." A male voice spoke to her.

"Sure, please send someone to the family room for me as soon as possible." She said and then I didn't smell or sense her nearby anymore.

Then I seen it, a bright light one at a time beaming into my eyes. Next, I heard the individual telling me if I could hear him and understand what he was saying then squeeze his hand as he picked my hand up.

Giving myself a little pep talk, I did it. I squeezed with all my might. Next, I began to blink my eyes until I was able to adjust them to the brightness of the overhead lighting in the room.

"Well hello Mr. Johnson. It is great to see you open your eyes. Don't try to talk. I'll send someone in here to remove the breathing tube and get you some ice chips. I'm afraid that your throat will be a little bit sore for a while. Now let me finish my examine. I need for you to blink or nod your head for me to let me know you feel certain spots on your body. Even though you were shot in your chest we still need to conduct this test. Do you understand those instructions.?"

I nodded my head, barely but I did. I was scared to close my eyes by blinking, scared they may stay closed again. I was relieved when I felt each place he ran the tip of a pen like object, nodding as he asked me if I felt it. Once the doctor finished with his examination, he ordered for a nurse to come remove the tube and bring me those ice chips. When the nurse had entered and began to take the tube out, Brenda walked in the room with a huge smile on her face. Her smile was so infectious, and I knew at that very moment that even if I didn't learn she was pregnant, just seeing her face would have stopped me from leaving her.

"Well hello sleepy head, so glad to see you have finally decided to wake up. I've missed you so much." She said.

I was still unable to respond and when the tube was removed I tried to speak but the pain in my throat made it impossible.

"Don't rush and speak to me. They told me if may take you awhile to find your voice." Brenda said not taking a seat next to the bed and held a cup with the ice chips inside. She slowly began to give me some and the coldness from them, meeting with the pain in my throat was soothing but not enough to take all the pain away.

"Baby." I barely got out

"Yes, I'm here." She answered.

"Not you. The baby." I couldn't form a complete sentence but I was trying to confirm that she was indeed pregnant with our first child.

"Marque, are you trying to tell me that Clover confirmed she is really pregnant? Brenda questioned.

Shaking my head, no, I lifted my hand and reached for her stomach. When I did that a single tear drop fell down her face. I moved my hand from her stomach to her face as I wiped that lone droplet of water and smiled.

"You heard me baby, and that's what caused you to open your eyes?"

"Yes."

"Then yes we are having a baby and I can't wait to live the life I have been dreaming about with you."

She was still feeding me ice chips bit by bit and I felt I could form a longer sentence, so I spoke up. "I'm sorry."

"Baby listen to me okay, there ain't nothing for you to be sorry for. You didn't do this to yourself. A trigger-happy police officer shot you. I don't understand how or why you was in a parking lot with Clover when you said you was going to her house to talk to her but that isn't important anymore. All I care about is you getting better and we carry on living life together."

"You're right, I didn't hurt myself. Your brother is the main reason why I am in this bed." I struggled to get out.

Brenda

To see Marque, awake and alert was an amazing feeling in itself but to know that hearing me tell him we created a life together was even better. It seemed like that was the driven force for him to come all the way back to us. Approximately an hour later just as he was really getting his voice back, in walked two officers. I stood up, assuming at first, they were coming to get a statement from him so imagine my reaction when I seen one pull out the little card they use to read someone their miranda rights.

"Mr. Marque Johnson, I am glad to see you pulled through. I am here to read you your rights…" as the officer began I pulled out my phone to call an attorney.

"What is he being charged with, I have an attorney on the phone?" I asked.

"Assault and battery on Clover Matthews and Assault and Battery on a police officer and resisting arrest." The other officer informed us.

"So, you mean to tell me my fiancé gets shot by a police officer, and without doing a proper investigation you just charge the victim? Is there any evidence supporting the allegations made by a distraught ex, oh and let me guess it was my brother Rob, who claims he was assaulted by Marque? Come on, aren't you guys tired of cleaning up his mess. My fiancé is innocent and I'm taking the whole department down with me while doing it. Remember my brother is dirty and a dirty cop talks to his girlfriend about the dirt he does while on the clock and with who." I told them truthfully.

"I don't know what you are referring to. I have no idea who

your brother is nor what took place landing Mr. Johnson in this hospital. I am just doing what my superior instructed me to do." One of the cops said back to me.

"We will have an assigned officer outside your room door until you are discharged at which time you will be transported to be arraigned in front of a judge." and with that they left out the room however one stayed standing just outside Marque's hospital room door.

I looked over at Marque and he had a look of fear plastered on his face. Resuming where I was sitting before they walked in, I grabbed his hand and held it. I loved this man so much. It's crazy how in just a few short months how he was able to just enter my life and take over my heart with little to no effort. I never saw myself loving another man as I had for Kareem. Rob had planted drugs in his car one night he was at the house visiting me, when he left to go to the studio he was pulled over and they found the large quantity. He's been in jail ever since and refuses to speak with me. That broke my heart and I vowed to never allow myself to love someone else in fear that Rob would strike again. Here he is, he did it again, this time he almost got my fiancé killed. I'm afraid of what he may do to him once he finds out I'm pregnant with Marque's baby.

"I'm going to pay for your lawyer. We are going to get this mess cleared up." I tried to reassure him.

"How can you afford to pay for a lawyer to help me with the job you have? Do you understand I have a conviction of murder on my record? No matter what the truth is, they are going to see a black man with a serious offense, a violent one at that, calling a white woman and a white officer a liar."

"Well maybe we can help you." I heard a strange voice from the doorway. I wasn't sure who this couple was standing now at the end of the bed with sympathy etched on their face.

When I looked to Marque to figure out who these people were, his eyes were glossing over. I knew he didn't really have any family left beside his grandparents, so I was dumbfounded on who this older couple was.

"Hello, Marque how have you been? Seeing as we couldn't get you to reach out to us when you returned to the states and we learned you was shot, we knew this was our opportunity to come see you. Wish it was under different circumstances." the man spoke up.

"Excuse me but who are you?" I asked, not trying to sound rude but I didn't understand who they could have been.

With his head held down, Marque whispered, "Ethan's parents."

"Boy lift that damn head!" the woman spoke with authority.

Doing as he was told, Marque now had tears streaming at a steady flow. Not caring that these strangers, at least to me were standing in the room, I got up and went to wipe the tears and placed a kiss on his cheek close to his ear to ask him if he wanted me to have them leave.

"I couldn't face you guys, it hurts not having him around." Marque spoke not answering my question, however speaking with a quiver in his voice to them.

"Hi young lady, would you mind if me and my husband had a few words with Marque? We want to catch up with him and offer to help him. We believe he is innocent." Ethan's mother said to me in a tone completely different than the one she used to demand Marque to lift his head.

I looked toward Marque and he just nodded. I gave him a kiss then walked out the room.

CHAPTER SEVEN

Marque

I have been avoiding seeing Esther and Erick because I couldn't come right out and tell them that I saw firsthand their son be blown to pieces. I feared they would ask me details. How can I describe what I try so hard to block out and forget.

"Now son, I'm not going to jump on your back because you pushed us away, at least not right now. We only want to know what landed you in this position so we can figure out the best way to get you cleared from the allegations then have you once and for all leave this god damn racist area." Erick stated.

I ran down the events of the past few months to them, starting with when Clover had lost custody of her children. I told them how

I got closure with my mother, with my demons from my childhood by revisiting the home I grew up in until the night I killed my father. When I got to talking about Brenda and how we were friends for years, and one night it was as if this warm magical feeling engulfed me and I just knew she was made for me, Esther's eyes were smiling.

"She is the one for you." Esther said before walking and sitting on the end of my bed, then added, "While you were just speaking of her your eyes lit up, your voice softened a bit. She is very beautiful son and lucky to have you."

"Thank you, Esther. I am sorry I never stayed in contact, it just is so hard to accept he's gone. He was the only person I had in life besides my grandparents and now Brenda." I stated.

"Wrong, you have a very large family, a family that has missed you a great deal. Now listen, I'm going to get the family lawyer on this. I'm going to do some inside work as well and see what I can find out about this brother of hers because it appears from what you told me that when these ridiculous charges are cleared he will remain a problem. Lastly, we would love it if you and your girlfriend will accept the invitation and move back into your condo, stay away from her brother as much as possible." Erick said.

"Why would you do all this for me?" I had to ask them. I mean I knew they were amazing people from the little time spent while living in Revere but that was years ago.

"We lost our only son Marque. Like you he didn't have many friends, most kids he went to school with choose to go the illegal route while he remained focus on making something of himself. You were the closest thing to a brother he had, plus we love you Marque as if you were family. Think about it okay?" Esther said.

"I will, I promise. Of course, I have to see what Brenda thinks about it. This is her home and outside of her brother she has an amazing family." I informed them.

"She loves you, she is going to want to be with you. Watch and you'll see." Esther said tapping me on the leg before she stood up and walked to embrace me.

"Thank you both for coming up here. Give Brenda, my fiancé who is also soon to be mother of my child your number to lock in her phone and I promise I will stay in touch. I'm feeling a little tired right now." I told them.

"Oh, my congratulations Marque, we are very happy to hear such wonderful news. I will be exchanging numbers on my way out with her, I'd love to get to know this woman." Esther said as she was walking towards the door.

Saying goodbye one final time they left out the room and a few minutes later in walked Brenda.

"They seem like a very nice couple." she stated.

"They are. They are going to have their family lawyer represent me and they want us to move to my condo I shared with Ethan once I am released." Looking at her as I said it trying to read her expression.

"I don't want to leave Melanie stuck not able to afford the apartment we share now." she replied.

"How if I offer to pay for your portion until she can find a new roommate. I agree with them, moving from here is best for me, even more so now that you are having my baby. Your brother is a problem and has the law backing him. Next time I may not survive."

"You are right, okay let's do it then baby, but where is it again?

60

How far of a commute will it be for me to get to work?"

"Just find a job closer to where we moving too. The condo is located right on Revere Beach." I told her.

"I love my job and the customers. I have a personal relationship with all the regulars."

"Well then I guess we have some thinking to do but I know I am going to move. I have a baby on the way now that I need to keep my black ass alive for and with a racist ass cop gunning for my life and freedom ain't no telling what his next attack on me will be." I didn't mean to sound so selfish but damn she couldn't begin to understand how I was feeling.

I had to be aware of my surroundings less when I was at war in a foreign country than I do in this town I lived in. My mind was made up, I am going to go back to the condo and start a new life. If she didn't want to move, then I respect her choice. She can decide for us to date long distance and see one another on weekends and co-parent once the baby arrived.

Clover

I was all healed up and feeling like I haven't in weeks on weeks. I don't know what I was thinking about jumping into traffic, well yes, I do, but it wasn't worth the broken ribs and two broken legs which needed a few surgeries. I haven't had one person come visit me the three weeks I have been laid up in the rehabilitation center. I missed my kids, I tried a few times to call and talk to them but Ed never answered my calls.

"Hello sunshine. You ready to break free from here.?" nurse Ashley asked me.

"Not really, everyone has been so kind to me, I'm afraid of what's to come once I walk out and I'm on my own."

"What are you so afraid of? Is it your ex-boyfriend that assaulted you just prior to being shot? If so, you know you can seek an order of protection against him." she said.

"No, I doubt he will come near me ever again." Shamefully I lowered my head.

I wasn't ready to talk about the events that took place, but I knew I needed to tell the truth on what happened. Marque all around was a good man, one who didn't deserve the fate handed to him. I couldn't see then what I know now due to the alcohol that flowed through my veins but laying up in this hospital bed did something to me. It was as if I was rebirthed and saw with a clear mind all of my wrong doings. I only pray that one day Marque can find it in his heart to forgive me with understanding that I was not in the right headspace. I was sick, alcohol had took over and I lost everything due to it. I was always a social drinker, a glass of wine with dinner but I stayed clear of the hard stuff up until my kids were ripped from my life. I enjoyed the warm feeling of the vodka as it made its way down my throat. I liked the cloudy floating like feeling that eased the pain that the effects of drinking a few bottles did. Had I not consumed so much in a short period of time I more than likely would have been able to see the signs that I was pushing a great man away from me.

"Do you need for us to set up any other services for you, follow up care of some sort?" Ashley inquired.

"Yes, perhaps if it's not too much trouble can you print up some local NA/AA meetings. I want to have access to those in case I feel like buying a bottle to drink my problems away."

"Of course, I will get that information and include it with your discharge paperwork. Clover you are a very bright beautiful girl. Don't beat yourself up over what took place. Use it as a platform to better your future. Get your life back all the way on track first, then you go fight for rights to your kids. Love can wait, don't look for it. Let it find you."

Ashley had became a good friend to me while I was laid up in this room. She listened to my problems, never judging me. She always left out the room leaving me with a good feeling and positive things to think about.

Two hours later the Uber was pulling up outside my building when I noticed all the windows inside looked bare, no shades or curtains. I grabbed the hospital bag filled with donated clothes for me to wear while in rehabilitation as I had no one to bring me up my own. I walked up to the outside side door that opened up to my apartment, which was an added bonus to living on the first floor. I put my keys into the lock but it wouldn't turn. I walked and looked into the window and noticed everything inside was gone. I fell down to my knees and began to sob. I have no idea where to go right now. I have no money, no home apparently, no family or friends. I took a few deep breaths, grabbed ahold of my bag. I began to walk slowly on the walking shoes that I was prescribed to wear while my legs still healed, up the long street to the police station. I needed to be directed to the closest shelter. I guess this was my karma.

It took me a good hour to finally reach the precinct. Inside I walked up to the partition and spoke through the glass that I was just discharged from a rehabilitation center and needed to be placed in a shelter. The woman behind the glass rolled her eyes and hit a few keys on the desktop computer in front of her, she then slid out the sheet of paper with 4 different public shelters, all of which were over 40 miles away.

"Do you think I could get a patrol car to bring me to one that has an opening? I have to two broken legs, I can't walk that far." I asked her.

"Ma'am it is not our job to transport anyone anywhere. Perhaps you should have stayed in detox then." Looking down on me she said.

"For your information, ma'am, I wasn't in that kind of rehabilitation center. I was injured in an accident. It appears while I was in the hospital healing, my landlord emptied my apartment and I have nowhere else to go." Just saying the words made it more real and I couldn't help the tears that fell from my eyes.

"Either way, ma'am it is not our job to transport you anywhere."

I felt so defeated. I wanted to go back to the rehabilitation hospital, lie and tell them my legs weren't okay. Tell the doctor I think I was released too soon to try and buy time until I could find somewhere I could move to. I was getting hungry. I stepped away from the glass window but slid down the wall and just began to cry, cry for many reasons but yet nothing at all if that makes sense. I wish I had died when I jumped in traffic.

CHAPTER EIGHT

Marque

Today is the day I go back to court for a probable cause hearing where a judge will determine if the prosecution has enough evidence for the case to move on to a pre-trial. Since my release I was let out surprisingly on my own personal recognizance. The attorney Esther and Erick had hired to defend me was very good at his job. Thankfully because I was sure I would be given a high bail. I had just finished sliding into my blazer jacket when Brenda yelled out for me to hurry up because now that we have relocated we had a long drive and had to go through Boston to get to interstate 91 to head out. That traffic in the morning was hell in this part of the state but the further out you went in any direction the lighter the traffic.

Two and a half hours later we were pulling up to the courthouse. I was nervous and I don't know why. I knew today I wouldn't be convicted either way, it wasn't a trial date. If anything I consider it to be a good court date, we will be presented with what the district attorney plans to use as evidence against me. I know that all they had was statements from a racist cop and a ex with a grudge. Brenda had walked in to the courthouse moments before me and they let her right through. The minute I went to walk through the metal detector, which didn't go off might I add, I was asked to stand off to the side so the court officer could use the wand to check me for weapons.

"Mr. Johnson, come on. I was waiting on the sidelines to see if you would be treated unjustly. I am Mr. Johnson's attorney, take my card. My client didn't set off anything when he went through the detector." My lawyer Mr. Romanovitz spoke with a tone in his voice where he dared for one of the court officers to go over him.

The court officer stepped to the side, never following through with his original plan of searching me more. I walked off this time with more confidence. I could tell that my lawyer is well known and not taken as a joke. On the elevator ride to the 3rd floor he informed me that he had hired an investigator on my behalf, who will be going out and questioning the witnesses that were on the scene.

We were in and out the courtroom. My name was called and the prosecution stated they had numerous witnesses that stated they heard the alleged victim scream for help that she was being assaulted. They also said many witnesses stated that from the looks of it I was wrestling the officer for his weapon during me resisting arrest. I couldn't believe the bullshit I was hearing.

Just as fast as we walked in the courthouse we were walking out. I stood outside with Mr. Romanovitz discussing the case, agreeing to get together in two weeks to discuss the case in more details once he would get a report back from the investigator. I walked to the car and before I climbed in I removed my jacket. Something told me to look around at my surroundings and thankfully I did because I noticed Rob, dressed down in and not riding in a city car parked up some ways from me. I hoped he wouldn't be dumb enough to try anything again, because this time he don't have a badge on.

Sliding in the car, I made sure to buckle my seatbelt and adjust my mirrors prior to starting the car. I told Brenda to do the same. We had made plans on going by the diner and seeing her friends before we headed back to the city, now I was wondering if that was a wise idea. I didn't want to let Brenda down so I brushed those thoughts to the back of my mind without mentioning them. I put my left directional on, letting the cars that were driving along the road know that I was about to pull out from my parking spot. Once I was driving at a steady 35mph as allowed by law on the road I was currently driving on, Brenda looked my way.

"Baby why are you sweating so much? Are you not feeling well?" she asked me.

"No, I feel fine, I didn't realize I was sweating. Don't worry."

"Then it's something that is bothering you, your body is stiff, you are watching the mirrors and the speedometer at the same time making sure you don't go anything over the speed limit."

"I see your very observant, aren't you?" I looked to her and asked.

"It's not hard to tell. Is it your nerves being back out this way?"

"Subconsciously probably. Let's just go on to the diner and have a nice slice of apple pie and some coffee. That will make me feel better. Maybe you can get your old boss to finally give you that recipe."

"Bruce is never going to kick in that recipe. He won't even tell his wife Margie." Brenda said laughing.

"While we are here, we need to go by your doctors and pick up a copy of your medical records to bring with us to your appointment next week. I almost forgot. We need to keep a close eye on my son now." I told her.

"You are really set on this being a boy? What if she is a mini me?" she shot back.

"I guess it's a battle of the sexes then. I say boy like his daddy, you say a girl like her mama. Either way my love is the same." I had wanted to lean over and give her a kiss. Every time we talk about the baby, a strong emotion takes over, the need to show her my love increases; however, I wasn't risking any reason for her brother to call one of his work buddies and have me pulled over. That is how this whole thing had started.

Brenda

It felt so good to be spending the day back in Athol. The way of life was much more private here, but I fully understood why Marque wanted us to relocate. I had sent my mother a text message letting her know that we were planning on stopping by the diner before heading back to the city, if they wanted to come see us.

The past few weeks have been good, besides dealing with Marque's frequent nightmares. He just started seeing a new therapist who was going to try him on a medication to help him with those. If anyone deserved to suffer from PTSD that brought on these violent nightmares, my man sure didn't. From killing his father at 12, to serving in a war and losing his best friend in front of him, and now being a victim of police brutality yet the courts were charging him with a crime not the officers who pulled the trigger.

We were in the diner for no longer than 10 minutes when I heard my name be called from behind, instantly the hair on the back of my neck were at attention. I felt Marque tense up as well. I slowly turned around on the bar stool I was sitting on and there he was. My brother the devil.

"What the fuck you want Rob? I have nothing to say to you." I spat.

"You're my baby sister, I love you and I just wanted to see how you were doing?" he replied.

"Excuse me, I'm going to go make a call outside." Marque said as he went to stand up.

"No, you sit right here. Don't let my bitch of a brother intimidate you. You're not suppose to be 100 feet near me. I am pretty sure you know the law, try abiding by it sometime."

"About that bullshit piece of paper, you had me served with. We are family it's not a good look Brenda. My co-workers are starting to look at me funny because of your false accusations. I'm on fucking desk duty because of all the bullshit you are telling people about me. You are ruining my reputation." Rob said, however I wasn't the least bit phased by his speech.

"Yeah well welcome to my life. You have had your head up your ass for way too many years, you have gotten away with countless crimes because of that badge. Maybe they should strip you of it all together. You got my fiancé, the father of my unborn child shot because of your personal vendetta against men of color. Now if you don't leave from here, I will have no choice but to dial 911 from my cell phone and tell your superiors that you are breaking a 209a order against you." As I reached in my purse to pull out my cell phone I made sure to pull out the pink piece of paper I was told to carry on me at all time. It was my order of protection against my brother I made sure I got that first day I learned Marque was shot.

"This ain't over!" he yelled as he stormed out the door.

"Do you want to leave, I understand if you do. I can always wait for another time to see my parents baby." I told Marque.

"No, we traveled all this way. We need to stop running from the problem and fight them head on. I'm not going to let him chase me away from living life. This is your hometown Brenda. We should be able to come and go as a couple without your brother taking control and chasing me off."

"You know I love you right?" I asked him.

"That I do know, If I know nothing else I know that you love me." Marque answered leaning over and giving me a kiss.

"Okay now children, that's how you got that one in the oven now." I heard my father say as he snuck up on me.

I jumped up from my seat and wrapped my arms around my dad. You see I was a full-on daddy's girl. We had an unbreakable bond, and he always sided with me. Rob hated that shit. He felt like fathers and sons were supposed to be the ones close and mothers and daughters stuck together. In our home, that wasn't the case. Growing up my mother gave equal amounts of love to the both of us, she didn't have a favorite the way my father clearly did. Once we hit our teenage years, my brother began to resent me. He used to pull some cruel pranks on me, putting Nair hair remover in my shampoo a week before Prom so I was forced to go buy a wig. What made it so bad is we live where the only wigs you could find was something someone's grandmammy would wear to church on Sundays. I had no way of proving that he did that because as I ran out the bathroom Rob snuck back in and took that bottle out and placed a Nair bottle in its place. My mother said I must have not paid attention and grabbed the wrong bottle. I was so relieved that I was going to be going to college in Connecticut because I would be away from him, away from home.

While I was away at school, is when I had met my ex. Kareem's major was in musical arts. He was thirsty to learn the ins and outs of the music industry. He had dreams of being big like P. Diddy but as I mentioned earlier, that all went down the drain when he left from visiting me on school break and was pulled over by my brother. While I was away in school, my brother had went to the police academy trying to impress my father, and it worked up until my brother pulled that stunt. My father knew my brother did something because unbeknownst to Rob, my father had just brought Kareem's car to his shop he owned to be detailed. My father knew was no drugs in the trunk of the car. It was then my brother was outcasted all the way. I know my mother meets with him here and there but as for myself and my father we cut ties with him. I actually had met Melanie from all that took place. They were dating at the time. She was scared to leave him, she sent me a message one day on Facebook telling me how she was afraid to leave my brother, and how he had confessed to her how he got rid of my thug boyfriend. I showed the messages to my father, who sped to the apartment they shared and he told her to pack up her stuff and come move in his house.

I always prayed that whatever fixation my brother had, he would wake up and realize that his actions was causing him to be the lonely miserable man he turned into. He really is an attractive young man. I told my parents when his behavior had started to shift that perhaps they should enroll him in some kind of therapy but back then I was the only one who noticed something was off with him. Growing up, I always imagined I would have a close relationship with my brother, my only sibling. I envisioned us getting married and our children growing up being best of friends not just cousins. Now that I am having a baby, one with a wonderful man who happens to be of a different ethnicity I know my visions will never happen. My brother will never be allowed near my child, I'll kill him before I let him hurt my child.

Not wanting to worry my parents, I never mentioned that Rob had popped up at the diner while I was waiting on them. We enjoyed lunch and made plans for them to come out to the beach and see what all the hype about Kelly's Roast Beef was. We had an extra room, granted in time we will be converting it to the baby's nursery but we kept Marque's old furniture inside until I got further along.

We said our goodbyes. Many, many hugs and handshakes took place between my parents, and my old co-workers with me and Marque collectively and we left out. Marque was now in better spirits from earlier, probably because he had a to go pie wrapped up as a gift from my boss. I guess I have to get use to not calling him my boss still but some things die slow. Marque had parked outside my doctor's office so I could just run inside real quick and grab the paperwork that was waiting for me at the front. As I was walking out, I was looking at some of the papers and didn't see someone coming in the office door until I bumped into the individual. It was none-other than Clover.

Clover

Opening the door to my new physician's office I walked right into a patient that also wasn't paying attention. I looked up to say sorry for being careless and not watching where I was walking when I realized it was the woman Marque was with. My eyes darted behind her, hoping I spotted Marque so I could perhaps have a talk with him.

"He ain't here so stop looking for my man. You caused enough problems Clover." this Brenda woman angrily said.

"I don't want any trouble. I was hoping to have a word with him, you can be there as well. I have some things I would like to speak to the two of you about. If that's okay?" I asked giving her a small smile.

Nervous is not a strong enough word to describe how I was feeling. I wouldn't be surprised if the medical assistants in the office didn't hear my heart beating rapidly as they were checking other patients heart rates with the stethoscope. My palms began to sweat, but neither of us moved, we stood frozen in the same spot we landed just looking at one another. Now that I am free of alcohol I can see why Marque was attracted to her. She was very beautiful.

"That won't be a good idea Clover. Do you know how bad I want to just catch a case right now by beating your ass? However, not only do I have a lot to lose but that will cause more damage to the case my fiancé has pending. So, if you will kindly step out the way so I can leave. We have a long drive to the city and we don't want to get stuck in the horrible traffic. This baby tends to get sick on long rides." she replied rubbing her small stomach where you could however tell she had something growing inside.

"Congratulations to the two of you, Brenda. I mean that. Can you at least tell Marque how very sorry I am for everything? I was told I will be summoned into court, however what I have to say which is the truth the whole truth and nothing but the truth, I'm positive he will have all charges against him dismissed." With that I stepped to the side so she could exit out and I could enter.

Going back real fast to the day I lost all hope, sitting on the floor in the lobby of the police department wallowing in my misery I was approached by an older woman who had came into the station to obtain a copy of a police report. She knelt down next to me and offered me a Kleenex to wipe my tears and nose with. She had asked me what was the problem and was there anything she may be able to help me with. I broke down even more and told the woman what had led me to be ready to give up on life. This angel, with a warm loving smile assisted I get back on my feet and offered to bring me to her family's bed & breakfast located in the town over. She told me that she actually had just picked up an accident report that took place a few weeks prior where her husband was in a bad accident and after many different code blues, he finally stopped fighting and passed away. She was left to handle everything at the business and could use some help, if I was willing to work for free for a trial basis helping with meal preparation and changing the linens on beds and simple stuff like that then I could occupy one of the rooms free of charge.

I wasn't sure what exactly I did to deserve this break but I was grateful and I made a vow to do any and everything I could to help Marque get off those charges they placed upon him, as well as try to help him get the justice he deserved for being shot.

Back in the present day, everything has been working out with my new living situation. Sue was such a sweet lady. Her and her husband, Charles I later found out his name, have 4 grown kids. They all live away from home with their wives and children. Sue, is actually the one who referred me to this doctor and I'm beginning to believe in fate. Fate had me meet her and now give me the opportunity to fix my wrongs. It has only been 2 short weeks since I have been staying with her but I was learning so much about running a business from home. Charles had converted the old barn they had on the land into a cute loft styled home for the two of them once the last of their children had moved out. Once that was done, he had the original house in which they raised their kids in converted into the bed and breakfast. Each of the 5 bedrooms had a small bathroom for sanitary reasons.

I was going to take this opportunity and second chance to live a normal happy life and work harder than I ever have at anything to make sure I didn't screw this up. Next thing on my to do list is to be able to go to court and file for visitation with Brock and Baily. I missed my minions so much. I've realized that they are truly my real loves and I was foolish for not taking Marque up on the offer to end things when my kids were at risk. I just never imagined that I would lose them to begin with. Marque had a great job and never harmed my children, I didn't see the judge handing my babies off to my ex.

"Mrs. Stiros follow me."

Hearing the nurse call me from the doorway that led to back, snapped me from my rambling thoughts. "Here, I come." I replied standing up and following her to get my follow-up and hopefully hear that the walking shoes I needed could now be another bad memory I can toss.

CHAPTER NINE

Marque

"Wow these are so remarkable!" Brenda's father Mr. Chandler said while looking at one of the large sandcastles on the beach. His wife was right next to him, snapping pictures like crazy. I glanced over at Brenda who was now sporting a belly that her shirts could no longer hide.

5 months has passed since I was shot and I learned I was having a baby. We had planned a gender reveal party for this weekend and Brenda's parents along with Melanie has came a few days early so they could see the annual sand sculpture event held on the beach. I had a surprise planned for Brenda tomorrow that was hard to keep from her but Esther and Erick have been a godsend to me. They have welcomed Brenda in with open arms like they did for me many years ago. The baby shower is actually taking place in their backyard.

They was covering the cost of everything.

I am back to work at the post office, but clearly one out here. It was so much easier. I wasn't frowned upon. Whenever me and Brenda would go to the mall shopping for gender neutral clothes, no-one stared at us with disgust because we were a in an interracial relationship. It's odd how we only moved across the state not across the country and the difference in how we was treated was completely opposite.

"I still can't believe I have never heard of this event. How do they keep it to hold shape? What happens if it rains while this goes on, it must ruin all the artist hard work." Mrs. Chandler said still taking tons of photos with everyone posed in front of each statue.

After a few hours of viewing all of them, and Mrs. Chandler using up all her memory in her phone on photos of the sandcastles, we walked to Kelly's so they could get a taste of some of the best seafood in the state. Brenda has an allergy to iodine so she couldn't eat shellfish, she opted to get a roast beef sandwich three way with some fries. We got our orders and crossed back over to the beach and took a seat at the benches to enjoy our food, outside. I felt Brenda nudge me and when I looked at her she nodded her head towards Melanie who was in a deep conversation with a hispanic man, just laughing and giggling.

"Can't bring you anywhere I see." Brenda said teasingly to Melanie.

"I'm just trying to find my Mr. Perfect, like you found yours." she replied, then turned back to carry on the conversation.

"Is everything all set for tomorrow?" Brenda then asked me.

"Now you know woman that they have everything covered. So, tell me again what do you want to name my son?" I asked her

"If it's a boy, and that is a strong if, I think it would be beautiful to name him Ethan, that is if Esther and Erick are okay with that." She stated.

"Really?" I asked her. I was shocked and a wave of emotion just took over me. Now more than ever did I want this woman to give me a boy.

"What about a girl, have you considered any?' she inquired.

"How about we name her after my mother?" I asked.

"Deal, either way we can honor the two closest people in your life baby that are no longer here." Once she finished saying that I went to kiss her but she moved away with the quickness.

"No kisses for you until you brush your teeth. I'm not trying to be walking around my baby shower with lips 10 times the original size."

We all broke out in laughter with her response including the dude Melanie was still talking to.

***

I must admit that Erick and Esther did an amazing job on the baby shower. The décor alone was amazing. Everything was blue and pink. I had given Esther the sex of the baby in a sealed envelope given to me at Brenda's last appointment. The only one who knew what we were having was Esther. A few of Brenda's friends and old co-workers had took the trip down to be here as well.

Esther had a bunch of games set up for the guest to play, she also made enough food to feed an army. I was standing around taking in everything around me. Many faces I didn't know at all, the rest however were all friends of Brenda's or her family members. I know she wanted a girl so she could dress her up, have tea time or whatever with her but I prayed every night I got my boy. I need to have my legacy to carry on my families history. My grandparents had to cancel last minute in attending the party due to the flu going around. My grandmother had gotten it and was sick in bed.

"What has you so deep in thought son?" Erick asked stepping up to me.

"Just looking around and it hit me; I have no family nor any of my friends here. I mean I only had Ethan as a friend but I really was living a closed in sheltered life." I responded.

"Listen Marque, what happened to your father was deserved. You may not of had a real father growing up but you do have a dad in your life. The day our son brought you home to introduce us to you, you became one of us. You have family, son. A large one as you can see looking around this yard. We are your family and don't you ever think otherwise. Now pick up your face so we can get to this reveal, then for the surprise to take place. Are you ready?"

"Yes, sir I am ready to see all that blue and know that a prince will be born." I smiled. We embraced in a way that a father and son would and for the first time in all my years of living, I can say I knew what it felt like to be wanted and loved by a father figure.

"May I have your attention. Please gather around. First, myself and my wife Esther would love to thank you all for coming out to our home today and help us welcome our grandchild into this world. Many here are family and are aware that we lost our boy years ago while he was serving over in Afghanistan. Just before he was deployed he brought Marque home and it was then we knew we had gained another son. Now, let's get the show on the road and see what exactly has been slow cooking in that tiny oven Brenda is sporting over there." Erick said.

Brenda walked over to where myself and her parents along with my newfound set of parents, I guess you can say to once and for all, find out what we were about to be parents of. As everyone was crowding around us, Melanie was handing out sparklers with lighters to all the guess in attendance. Everyone made a huge circle around me and Brenda after Esther had positioned us back to back not facing one another.

"Okay is everyone ready to light their sparklers?" Esther said enthusiastically. Once everyone shouted out that they were she began to count to 3.

"One, Two, Three!". At that moment everyone lit their sparklers and for the first 30 seconds they burned white until I began to notice a hint of blue. Not long after that, I turned around and gave Brenda a huge kiss and thanked her for my baby boy. We stood in the middle of a now heart shape of loved ones with blue smoke and sparks flying.

"Brenda, this may not be what you had in mind but was no way I could think of a perfect moment in time other than here and now for you to take my last name. Will you do me the honor and say I Do today?" I asked now on bended knee.

"What about my dress?" she replied.

"That dress is just a dress baby, sell it. Let our baby be born in two months with parents who share the same last name. Let me make sure that you will be taken care of in the event trial don't go in my favor. We can always renew our vows later on down the line. I love you Brenda and I'm going to ask one more time, will you please take my hand in marriage today?"

"Yes Marque. I will never question you or your reasons for pushing it up." she said before pulling me up and kissing me.

80

Clover

My first overnight visit with Baily and Brock was tonight. As excited as I was, the nerves had me messing up all I had to do in preparation for them. Sue had showed me where she placed the cots for when a couple would stay with a child. She even had small portable cribs in the storage area. Not the pack-n-play yards but mini cribs.

I wanted to cook them one of their favorite dishes but I had spilled a whole pan of cooked pasta on the floor because I wasn't paying attention. I had grabbed the pan from the stove without pot holders. Thankfully, I didn't burn up my fingers. I cleaned up the mess, tossed the noodles in the trash, and put water on to boil to make a new box. Sue has taken me once a week over the past 2 months to visit with them at a agreed upon location. It was the kids that begged and pleaded to come sleep over. Ed wasn't on board at first until Sue assured him that it would be just her, me, and the kids at the house. She would shut down the bed and breakfast if it made a difference. I guess it did.

The next day

With me being able to spend time with my children, without Ed watching us like a hawk, felt amazing. We laughed, played a bunch of games then we changed into some jammies. We invited Sue over to the main house to see if she wanted to join us in a movie night. She declined reminding me that it was my time with the kids. All the work of pulling out cots and making them up with clean bedding was all for nothing. They both climbed in bed with me and we passed out as soon as our heads hit the pillow. I swear I had gotten the best sleep last night than I have in about a year when they first was ripped

81

from my home. I swear the time had flown and next thing I knew Ed, was out in the driveway tooting his horn. Giving them a big kiss and hug, I reassured my crying babies that the next sleepover will be for a full weekend.

Seeing the car take the left at the intersection a few houses away, I never noticed the black sedan that pulled in from the other direction.

"Clover?" a man with a polo type striped shirt and plain khakis asked.

"Perhaps, who is inquiring?"

"Hello, I'm an investigator hired by the lawyers representing Marque Johnson in an upcoming trial set for next week. I was wondering if I can steal a moment of your time and ask you a few questions.?"

"Um, sure that's fine, come on inside. Can I get you something to drink, water coffee?" I asked trying my best to remain calm. What could this man be trying to learn that wasn't already in the paperwork the lawyer had.

"No thank you. I just finished off my second Dunks so far. I promise this will be quick and then you can get back to your day. Do you recall the events of February 21st at approximately 4:30 in the afternoon?'

"Of course, I remember what took place that day. How could one forget." I replied.

"Very well, can you tell me what led to you and Mr. Johnson having to park and what led up to the alleged assault he committed against you?"

"I was in a bad place. I don't want anyone to hate me. My children were ripped from my care, my home. I turned to alcohol to cope with the depression. Marque had left me during my darkest moment in life for another woman, so put yourself in my shoes for one minute. When he showed up to the house that afternoon I just knew he changed his mind. We were going to fix our relationship. We left to go talk and Marque stated he didn't want to be inside of my home. During our conversation he pulled over and told me he was bringing me to get help. I don't understand what made me do it but I believed I was pregnant. I began to flip out, hitting myself all over screaming at him to stop while yelling for help. Someone had heard my cries and called the police. What took place next was something out of a movie. The officer began beating on Marque until backup arrived, he pulled his weapon from his its holster and made it look like Marque was fighting him for it, that is when the cop fired. I didn't mean for any of that to happen. I thought perhaps he would be arrested and spend a little time in jail." Now sobbing I looked up at the investigator.

"Ma'am will you be willing to testify in court and repeat what you just told me?"

I nodded my head yes. That was my plan once I detoxed and was thinking with a clear head.

"Are you aware of when the court date is, or should I have you summons to appear?" he asked me.

"I was already served a paper to appear from the district attorney office. I was going to tell the truth that day in court.

FINAL CHAPTER

Marque

"You are free to go Mr. Johnson. All charges against you have hereby been dropped. On behalf of myself and the county of Worcester Massachusetts I sincerely apologize to you for all you have had to endure. Upon the newfound information provided to this court, alongside the testimony given to this court from multiple witnesses that have come forward I will assure you that charges will be filed immediately not only Officer Bradshaw but Officer Chandler as well. Now as for you Miss Clover Stiros, I understand that at the time you were under the influence of a controlled substance being of alcohol but the poor choices you made that afternoon not only caused a great deal of trouble for Mr. Johnson, but you wasted taxpayers money and it has also been brought to my attention that your actions following the incident with Mr. Johnson caused a fatal accident, you will also be facing charges, please remain in the courtroom so we can go ahead and arraign you. Good luck to you

Mr. Johnson."

I couldn't believe that all this was happening. I turned around getting ready to walk out the courtroom when my gut told me to take a seat with the audience, so I could see what her outcome was. While Clover was on the stand repeating what she had told the investigator Mr. Romanovitz hired, she was the Clover I had first met. She had changed her life around, and now her life was crumbling down all over again.

"Fatal accident?" I heard the older woman who had entered the courthouse with Clover say while a distraught Clover looked at her.

"What was the date of this accident and where exactly?" she had asked no one in particular.

"February 21st, 2017 at the intersection of N. Main and Webster why?" Clover answered. I was still watching.

"Oh my God, it was you? You were the drunken fool who jumped in front of my husband's truck causing him to crash head on into that pole, it was you that ripped my husband from my life when we had so many plans."

"I'm so sorry Sue, I had no idea anyone else had got hurt besides me until just now. Forgive me please. You are all I have outside of my kids in my life." Clover began to cry uncontrollably.

Seeing enough, I stood up, grabbed my very pregnant wife and exited the courthouse. I said a silent prayer for Clover, I know many don't agree with me, but everyone deserves a second chance and a little praying over including Clover. As for Rob, I wouldn't care if they tossed his ass in jail and lost the key. The other officer, he was only doing his job as far as I could tell. He had no reason to doubt his fellow officer when he yelled for help. I wanted to close this chapter of my life and be able to move on.

Two weeks later

Picking up the baby monitor, I watched as my wife glided in the chair singing softly to our perfect son Ethan Johnson, no middle name needed. He has been home with us for a week now and everything has been nothing short of amazing. Ethan was such an excellent baby, he only fussed when he was hungry or needed changing. I stretched then slid out the bed and walked into the bathroom to take care of my morning needs. Walking out the bedroom, I made my way to my old room when I felt a presence. Knowing it wasn't anybody but Ethan letting me know he was watching over all of us, especially his namesake. I pushed open the door to the nursery quietly. I bent down to give my wife a kiss before taking my son out her arms.

"Go on and get ready for your first day back in college baby. I have him."

Brenda just smiled before leaning and kissing Ethan on his cheek then headed to our room to get dressed. I told Brenda after we got married that I wanted her to go back to school and no longer worry about what her brother may pull next. She was a grown, happily married wife whose husband will protect her come hell or high water.

I remained standing, swaying slowly until I knew Ethan was knocked out. I walked back into my bedroom and placed him in the cradle we had. We only brought him into the nursery when it was in the middle of the night and he needed to be fed and changed, that way the other parent could sleep until it was their shift.

THE END

Runnin'

PROLOGUE

The music was putting me to sleep. I hated when Damon wanted us to do these couple things. I didn't like any of his friends, well except for my brother. We were out on a cruise of the harbor with his cousin Trell and his date. Another delusional female, chasing a bag. It was clear she really wanted to dig her hands into my man's pocket and not so much his cousins. She was laughing at shit that wasn't even funny that Damon said, she was eye fucking the shit out of him and it was taking my all not to toss her ass over the side railing as if we were a part of the Boston Tea Party. I was about to tax that ass, but then I remembered what happened every time I reacted to things I didn't like. I'd go home and get fucked up for embarrassing him. He let it be known I am to be seen not heard. I figured it would be better if I walked off while they talked about childhood memories the men shared when Trell visited Jamaica where Damon was from. I have heard those stories each double date we had with Trell and the new bitch on his arm.

I was admiring the Boston skyline for a good half hour when I felt the tight grip on my arm and knew that later tonight I would pay but for what this time I'm not sure.

"Lynique what the fuck is wrong with you now? Fix your face and bring your ass back over there and act like you want to be here. I mean if you don't want to, next time I'll find a bitch to spend money on." He said low enough where only I could hear, then he leaned in and pecked me on my cheek for show.

I just smiled to go along with him and nodded my head, telling him I had to go use the restroom first. Finally letting my arm go he walked back over to Trell and his date and I headed for the restroom. Stepping out the stall I was washing my hand when this girl walked in laughing over her shoulder not paying attention. I had hoped she walked into some shit to teach her ass to pay fucking attention.

"Oh, here you are, I was just asking where was you at?" she said striking up conversation, one I didn't want any part of.

"I was feeling a bit sea sick, so I came in to get myself together. I'll see you back out on the deck." I stated trying to get out the way.

"You know how lucky you are to be Damon's date?"

"I'm not his date, I'm his girlfriend. This isn't just one night for me, this is one out of 7 days in a week I get to be around him. He is an amazing man ain't he. So easy on the eyes as well and girl what he does in the bedroom will leave your head spinning, but word of advice, keep your fucking eyes to yourself or it will be your ass. Now I must get back to my man, you hurry up and get back to your one-night date with his cousin, you just one of many."

I knew it wasn't her fault really, I mean Damon was a great catch in many ways. He was a boss and looked the part. Dark skin, tall and clean cut. He had a nice thick, solid physique that woman couldn't help but to trace along it with their eyes. His smile was bright, and the whites of his eyes were just as white as his teeth. He didn't smoke and barely drinks. I lived a good life with him for the most part. I wanted for nothing at all. Most times I had the latest fashions being delivered to my door before they even hit the shelves. The sex was out of this *world and he made me feel untouchable. Like I was made just for him. Sounds like the life right… well like the saying goes, all that glitters ain't gold. Damon has a side to him many aren't aware of, just me him and the walls of our home.*

Finally, after 2 hours, the boat had docked and we all parted ways. I glanced over and saw the jawline of Damon's face moving and I knew he was deep in thought. I only hoped it was about business and he had forgot about me walking off tonight. I knew once the door to our bedroom closed I would know for sure. Pulling into our driveway, Damon turned the car off and got out. He circled the car, opening my door and helping me out. Once inside I went directly to our room to prepare for what may come or may not. He was so unpredictable. As I was undressing I got sick again, so I ran for the bathroom and everything in me came up. Standing up and rinsing my mouth out, I decided to take a shower first. Normally I would see what his plans were because being beat while wet was not a good feeling. That was a greater torture, but I wasn't feeling too well for the past few days and I needed to take a shower.

Thirty minutes later, I stepped out and the house was quiet. I wrapped a towel around me, slipped into some house shoes and made my way to the bedroom. Once I entered I found Damon knocked out in the bed, or so I thought. As soon as I put on some panties and a nightshirt I pulled back the blanket on my side of the bed and he jumped up.

"Oh, did you think I was going to let you get away with embarrassing me tonight?" he asked me

"I just wanted to see the view, that's all baby. Can we just go to sleep, I'm not feeling well?" I pleaded.

"You must think I am dumb to believe that shit. I would have if while you were in the shower I didn't get a phone call from my cousin telling me he ain't get no pussy because of whatever bullshit you put in that girls' head tonight."

"I didn't tell her anything but the truth. Maybe she should have been real with him. You were the only reason she was on that boat. She wanted to get close

to you like all them other whores and she was using his dumb ass."

Wack.

There is was, he smacked me so hard, I swear I had whiplash. I picked my hand up to touch my face, when another slap came and hit me on the other side of my face. This time I felt blood trickle down my face from my nose.

"Damon, please baby not tonight. I really don't feel good. I keep getting sick." I pleaded but I was sure it would fall on deaf ears.

"You weren't thinking bout that when you were on that boat acting up. I chose you to be mine for a reason, to be a queen to a king. To stand beside me with pride."

"I wasn't trying to." Before I could carry on and beg, I felt dizzy and before I could catch myself I fell with everything blacking out around me. That saved me from getting my ass beat for real. I woke up to me laying in the bed, a cool cloth on my forehead and Damon sitting on the edge of the bed worried.

"I'm sorry baby. I should have listened when you said you wasn't feeling good. You scared me when you just fell like that. Go ahead and get rest. We will talk tomorrow." He bent down and kissed me.

The next day, I woke up and he was already gone. I slid out the bed and before I was stable on my feet I had to run for the bathroom, I felt sick. After a good 10 minutes dealing with dry heaves. I knew what the problem was. I climbed over to the bathroom closet and looked on the bottom shelf way in the back and pulled out the EPT test. Getting on my feet, I walked back to the toilet this time with an opened pregnancy test ready to find out what I already knew.

Seeing the word "pregnant" across the digital screen was all I needed to see to know what I had to do and fast. I didn't even bother to shower. I rushed out the room and packed me two good size bags of clothes. I went to the safe and pulled out all my jewelry along with 500k in 100 dollar bills that Damon had inside and I walked out the door, leaving my phone right on the bed. I got in the waiting Uber and had them drop me off at South Station. I boarded a train to Brockton, where I found a dealership and bought a cheap little car to get me out of here. With temp plates I drove to Providence where I got me a room to sit and think about what exactly I was going to do next.

CHAPTER ONE

Lynique

Taking this dreadful trip to the city already had me in a sour mood. Why did I make a promise to my family that this year I would spend the New Year with them? It's been about 5 years since I've left home and for a good reason. Living two hours away has given me the peace that I needed in my life, the peace I wanted back home for years but couldn't get. I only went back twice and each time it was to bury my nieces, other than that I stayed away. This time of the year was Esther's favorite so to help ease the empty feeling or try to fill a void I should say that my family was feeling, I packed a suitcase and locked up my home and made plans of spending two weeks with them, to celebrate a late Christmas.

See, I have a past I wanted no part of anymore. I moved away purposely to stay clear from my old life. I wanted nothing to do with

94

the people from my past, but I know that I will be face to face soon enough with the main one that I was running from, HIM, which is who I started to refer to Damon as. HIM being the one who destroyed my life in more ways than one. It took me years to build myself back up and heal from that heartbreak that he caused me. While I am driving up 93N my eyes are glossed just from the thoughts of the past 5 years wanting to pack up the life I have been living now and go home.

Damon, is his name and he's someone that fits the saying *when they love they love hard* and his love is of the dangerous kind. It's true I never had a man that catered to me the way he did and I wanted for nothing. Our love making sessions we're out of this world, it was like our bodies were made for one another, we just fit together like a hand in a glove. I believe he knew my body better than I did.

Leaving him was ultimately the hardest decision ever, because as I said a love like his is indeed a dangerous one. Just as much as he made me feel like no one was above me, he also made it clear to me I was his by putting his hands on me over his own insecurities. For example, he loved for me to dress up and he would show me off, but if another man's eyes lingered on me for a second too long then I would pay for it that night. I was very attractive, so I have been told all my life. I stood 5'4" and weighed 150. My weight was in all desirable areas. My breasts were just the right size for Damon to cuff, my waist small. My hips were wide with a round ass to match my thick thighs. I was not a light bright but not chocolate, I guess you can say I was like a chocolate milk complexion, I took care of my skin, so it was flawless with a natural glow. I never had the need to cake on makeup. Some simple mascara, eyeliner and lip gloss was just fine. I kept my hair in its natural curly state where it reached just past my shoulders. With that said, men always did more than glance in my direction, they would stare with their mouths open and Damon would remind me in a non-loving way that I was his only. To avoid an incident from taking place I would try to wear something less revealing, but he would demand I wear what he picked out, and I dreadfully would oblige and put on what he desired, knowing that later that night it would end with me coward in a corner of our room as he rained blows upon my body, making sure to avoid my face, at least most of the time.

I had to calculate and plan my way out the relationship and it took me over a year but once I got away I knew I had to stay away. Stay away from even my family because they were close with him, my same family that I kept all those beating from. I had to stay away because the way he would look at me I knew he would have me right back wrapped around his finger. That look was a power that he has always had over me and being that I never moved on and the fact that my heart still very much so yearned for him was all bad. I have a secret that I hid from all of them, one that I know will make it impossible once revealed for my life that I have lived for the past 5 years to continue the same.

When I did come home for the funeral's I did so from a distance, no-one knew I had came. I snuck in the church and hid in the back and would leave before it was over and return to my new life.

When I left, originally, I had no contact with anyone. It didn't take long for Damon to find someone new. I'm just hoping enough time has passed and that the bond he has with whoever she is, is strong enough that he won't bother me, even though many nights I would lay in my bed longing for his touch, I know I can't go back.

I pulled into my brother's driveway, sat in my car to gather the strength I knew I was going to need to get out and face reality and reveal a huge secret to everyone. Taking a deep breath, I got out and nudged a sleeping Jr in my back seat. That's right, my secret is when I left, it was to save my child. Had I stayed I know that it would only take one incident, one time for Damon to have a blackout and I could possibly miscarry my baby from a beating. I wasn't willing to sacrifice the life of my unborn child for the love I had for a man regardless if I had to raise my kid alone while mending a broken heart. I was already in the process of looking for a solid reason to leave and knowing I was with child was all the reason I needed.

As I went to knock on the door, it opened and although I knew I would be seeing Damon eventually during my time here, I wasn't prepared for it to be on the first day. The look on his face once he seen our son beside me sent shivers up my spine. When I tell you that our son looked like every bit of his father I mean that shit, and Damon didn't have to ask me who the little boy beside me was, he knew off rip that I had a baby from him and he never knew. His eyes turned black, his nose was flaring out and I noticed the veins popping out in his neck.

"Let me explain before you lose your cool Damon, and I hope you keep it together in front of him?" I said nodding towards Jr.

"Lose my cool, you are lucky my son is right here, and everyone is inside already, but we have all week to straighten this out and know that you will be answering to me, believe that." With venom in his voice he replied to me while stepping to the side to let us step in. He grabbed ahold of my upper arm with force and stopped me before I could enter the family room.

"You know you aren't leaving here with my son. You can go back to whatever you were doing, wherever you have been, and with whomever, but he will be staying right here with me."

"He is all I have and I'm not leaving him anywhere. Like you said we will talk later." I said as I yanked my arm from him and rushed in the room everyone was sitting in just staring at Jr.

CHAPTER TWO

Lynique

After hours of being interrogated about Jr and why would I keep him away from family but even more so his father, I couldn't do anything but say the same thing repeatedly, I don't know or I can't say why or it was hard to explain but I had my personal reasons.

If my brother had known that Damon was doing all that he was doing back then he would want to fight him, I'm his baby sister and he always protected me growing up. Every fight I had at the playground, he would be right next to me making sure it was a fair fight. The bond we have is insane but if he knew that his connect was laying hands on me a war he couldn't handle would erupt and it would all end bad. Bad for him because he was the breadwinner in his family, he was the sole provider who put dinner on the table and paid the bills, bad because he didn't have the same man power as Damon and bad because no one on the East Coast had product as raw as my ex.

After some time passed and the questions, the subliminal remarks degrading me as a parent keeping her child from family and the father, Damon finally spoke up in my defense.

Damon said to everyone "I let power get to my head. I thought I had Lynique right where I wanted her to always be but as we all know that wasn't the case because she got fed up and walked away, robbing me of being in my son's life." Well I thought he was going to do the honorable thing, but at least he took some of the blame.

"Wanting your woman to respect you is no reason for you to be robbed the way she clearly has robbed you of being in your son's life baby." his bitch that was sitting next to him spoke.

"Listen La Vida Loca unless you were a fly on the walls in my home that I shared with my son's father shut the fuck up. You want to speak up fuck it Damon let's do this, because I am tired of being a single mother. Tired of not having the answers to the questions my son asks about his dad. I'm also tired of the lie you had me living. Damon was kicking my ass for years and as soon as I sat on that toilet and seen that positive test I packed up and took what I needed from the safe to save my child no our child's life and I have zero regrets about it and I would do it all over again right now if I had to. You was so unpredictable that I wasn't risking you hitting me too hard or shoving me into a wall causing me to miscarry"

"Womp Womp Womp bitch you had a good life, so what you got a smack here and there. You probably deserved that shit anyway." this bitch spoke up again.

This hoe is going to learn today. I lunged across the table that separated us and grabbed ahold of her long bleached blonde hair and pulled her down. We both was on the floor as I straddled her taking all my hurt and frustration out on her that I have felt over the years for him, him being Damon. I felt someone grab me and automatically thought it was my brother breaking up the altercation like he use to do at the playground, but it was Damon not Tino. Seeing him with both hands on me and grabbing me brought me back to those horrible beatings he use to put on me and I began to really flip out.

"Let me fucking go, you will never put your hands on me again!" I screamed trying to break free. As this was happening his bitch got up from the floor and got in a lick while I was off guard.

"Oh, you, weak hoe, you got to sneak and hit bitch." I screamed while trying to break out of the bear hug Damon had me in.

"Mama why are you fighting?" just hearing Jr's voice instantly calmed me down.

"I'm sorry baby, go on and say bye to your cousins. We going home, this was a bad idea to even come here." I said with my chest heaving up and down.

"Lynique, I meant what I said when you got here, you want to run go ahead as much as I loved you then and still do I will never chase after you just as I didn't chase you 5 years ago, pussy comes a dime a dozen as you see you just fucked up one of many bitches I'm fucking, but you ain't leaving with my son."

"I'm not staying here with you and this bitch or any bitch for that matter. You want to get to know our son then you will do so without confusing him with a bunch of other women being around,

101

but trust me in two weeks we, me and my son, are going back home, home being our house, where you don't live and if this visit goes well we can come up with an agreement for the future with visits. I had every intention of having you meet him during my trip, just wasn't expecting it to be today."

It was then that Jr ran up to me and hugged my leg, "Mama you mean it, I can finally get to know my daddy?" then he turned toward Damon and said, "Hi, daddy. My name is Damon too but my mama calls me Jr because she said it hurts her heart to call me my daddy's name."

When he said that it broke me down. Not once did I think about how keeping him a secret and away from all his family but even more so his father would affect him. The one person I ran from, to protect him from is the very person I can see he missed having in his life. I had hurt my son, and I was regretting keeping him away as long as I have.

"Yes son, if everything goes good then you can come back on vacations but let's not rush it just yet okay." I said bending down and giving him a kiss on his head.

"Aye listen we bout to go, me, you and my son. I'm not sure where but tonight is for me and him and I want him to be comfortable so will you be coming with us?" Damon said.

"That stops right here right now, you can't order me around I'm not yours anymore. Tell her what to do, but don't demand me to do anything." I said as I pointed to his girl who was nursing a nose bleed.

"Bitch you can leave now." She spat.

"No bitch you can. This woman is my wife and will always come before anyone." Damon said.

"Oh, she get the wife title but never stuck around when it got tough to go through with the actual wedding, okay Damon, whatever you say. I'm gone."

I laughed but deep down inside I loved hearing that, I was in love with this man and I was beginning to think what harm could come from me spending the night with him somewhere and hell maybe even letting him have his way with my body one last time. It's been years and I have been craving his touch since the night I ran off.

CHAPTER THREE

Damon

As I am driving, doing my all to keep calm I keep glancing at my son sitting in the back seat with wide eyes looking at the skyline of downtown Boston at night. He was amused which lets me know that he was living somewhere completely different than the city. I was planning on using little pieces like that to figure out where he lived and what kind of life he had.

"How about we stop off at GameStop and get you something to do tonight once we get back from the movies?"

"That's okay daddy, I have my tablet in my backpack. Mama says that those kinds of games at GameStop are for bigger boys and girls and I only play on it for 2 hours. I'm not 5 yet, when I turn 5 she said I can play it for an hour longer." He replied.

104

I had to give it to Lynique, she is a good mother. I was impressed she wasn't the kind of new age mother that has the games or TV watch the kids while they bullshit on social media. Plus, my son spoke clear and was well mannered.

"Well that is good to know. What else do you like to do Jr.?" I asked because my house really didn't have much for a kid to do. It was basically a bachelor pad.

"I play with toys, but they are all at my house. Mama can daddy read to me tonight instead of you when we go to bed. You can come too if you want?" Jr had asked looking at Lynique in the passenger side of my car.

"Yes, your dad can read you a book." Lynique answered him then turned to me. "I tell him all the time books are food for the brain and he has to feed his if he wants to be successful."

"Even though I shouldn't be thanking you because you kept him from me I appreciate the way you are raising him. I never wanted a kid to grow up like I did, not having a real childhood because of bad choices my parents made."

I never really told her about my upbringing back in Jamaica. My father was a kingpin and my birth mother I never met because she was a maid he cheated on his wife with. I heard his wife tried to make my mother leave, but my father wouldn't have it, but once I was born my mother was never seen again and his wife had no choice but to accept me. The thing is she never did, at least not when my father was gone. In front of him you would think she adored me but the minute he walked away came the step mother from hell. She couldn't beat me and leave marks in obvious places because my father would notice, but she put hands on me, sometimes in places she had no business touching. I was 12 when she first sucked my dick. By the time, I hit 18 and could leave on my own I did that, using coming to the States to take over my uncle's business as an excuse. I hated my mother for being a coward and not standing up taking me with her. I hated my step mother for doing things to me all those years which is why I had no respect for Lynique and treated her like shit while I had her.

What she doesn't know is when she left I began to take a long look at what I did to make her run off like she did. I guess because my step mother never leaving my father left me the impression that if I loved her and gave her the world she would always stay with me. It was immature I know now to think that good dick and expensive gifts would be enough to keep Lynique but I learned the hard way, it took more than that to hold a real one down. I really do love her and if she is willing to come back I will try to keep my hands off her and that's my word.

I pulled into my driveway and seen that my son and Lynique both fell asleep. I guess she thought I still lived close to Boston, but I had moved to a small town in Rhode Island. I got out my car, closing the door quietly and running to unlock the front door then went back to the car opening the back door to get my son out first. I carried him into the house, up the stairs and placed him in a bed in the guest room that I was now planning on transforming into his own room. When I made it back to the car and seen Lynique was still asleep with her mouth slightly open, just like she always slept when she was exhausted, I decided to grab Jr's backpack and walk to the passenger side of the car to wake her up, so we can go inside.

"We here." I said softly nudging her.

"Where is Jr?" she groggily said getting out the car.

"I already carried him inside and put him in a bed."

I grabbed her hand and led her inside, bypassed the whole

downstairs and led her to my room. I had some things to discuss with her and what better place than the bedroom right?

"Where are you taking me Damon? I want to go sleep with Jr?"

"Not tonight you aren't, we have some making up to do, I haven't had pussy anywhere close to yours since you ran off and I know you miss this dick so we going to get reacquainted. It's going to be a long night so I hope that nap was a good one."

Lynique just looked at me, I knew she wanted it just as bad as I needed it.

CHAPTER FOUR

Lynique

The way Damon was staring into my soul was the image I had locked in my memory. I would close my eyes every chance I got and envision that look as I would use my vibrator that I searched high and low for when I was first living alone. I wanted the perfect one, as close to real as I could find, and I needed it to match his size and complexion, so it would feel right. At first, I had bought one and I thought, *what difference would the size make*, but it really made a big difference. I ended up putting it down and just used my fingers because it just couldn't fulfil my fantasy. The day I came across Twin, as I called my toy I jumped for joy in the store with people looking at me crazy. I called out of work the next day and stayed in bed for hours while my son was in daycare, just pleasing myself repeatedly while I pictured Damon being the one fucking me.

Just like the night he took my virginity, in the blink of an eye, before I was aware of what was going on, my clothes were off, and I was on my back in the middle of his big luxurious bed except tonight it wasn't my first time and I knew what to expect. His face was buried in my pussy and all I could think about was how much I missed his head game. I instantly came, and I knew from the past that he was just started. It didn't take long before I felt my legs trembling as I came again, but still, he didn't let up. I tried to run due to the sensitivity that was lingering from the powerful back to back orgasms I just experienced but he had a tight grip on my waist not letting me get away. I knew the only way to get him to stop was to allow him to bring me right back and quench his thirst, so I did just that, cummin' one more time as he came up smiling and licking his lips.

"I never got that sweet taste out my mouth." He said.

He was crawling up and getting into the position where he could enter me but didn't have any protection in hand, so I placed my hand on him and said "No way am I allowing you to enter me without using a condom. I don't know who you have been laying up with, seeing as I thought you had one woman and I learned today you balance out multiple, not to mention I'm not on birth control."

"Move your hand Lynique. I strap up every time I sleep with someone, I don't even allow them to suck my dick unprotected but now that you bring it up maybe I need to. I don't know who you been laying up with all these years."

When he said that I could see the wheels turning and I didn't want this to go left and have it turn into me being hit, so I quickly answered. "I haven't been with anyone since I walked out the doors of the home we shared Damon. My focus has been on our son and I wasn't going to be bringing no man around him when his father never knew he existed."

109

Just by saying that I could see the tension he was feeling simmer back as he leaned down and kissed me. This kiss was different than any other kiss we have ever shared. It was like he had a point to prove. With my mind now centered around this kiss he took it upon himself to enter me, and yes raw.

"You for real huh Lynique? No one been in my pussy, this shit is just as tight as that first night. You remember that night baby. You promised me you would always be by my side, but you lied to me, you ran off and many people had to pay for that." He said getting angry.

Damon began to punish my body, but it was feeling so good. My eyes were rolling to the back of my head. I couldn't think of a response right then, but I suppose we will need to talk after this.

"I'm not letting you go Lynique. Tell me what you want from me?"

He was moving in and out but at a slow pace now, our bodies were connected but the way we were staring at one another our souls reunited after years being apart and I was in my happy place. I loved this side of Damon, he was attentive, nurturing and I knew whenever we were intimate that he loved me just as much as I loved him. He showed me with each thrust, even when he got rough, his eyes would look into mine with a softness to them, evening it out.

"I can't stay. I don't want this to confuse you, but I have a life that I love and it's no longer with you." I said as I felt a tear slip out my eye.

"Then why is your eye crying for me. You know just as much as I do that together is where we need to be."

"I used to know that but not anymore. Let's not ruin this night." I told him.

For another 15 minutes, he made love to me, then just as I was reaching my climax he pulled out and laid on his back.

"For years, I told myself when I found you I was going to hurt you, when I seen you had my son my first thought was to kill you and take him and move home to Jamaica but my love for you outweighs the anger I have and while you are here I will show you I can be the man you wanted me to be all those years ago."

"Our time here isn't enough time, let it go." I said but once I finished saying that, the same mouth that uttered those words, wrapped themselves around his dick.

CHAPTER FIVE

Damon

"So, you just going to use me for my, ah shit that feels so good baby." I just continued to lay back and let Lynique do her thing. I swear she is a dick sucking pro. I taught her just how I liked it and I can see that she hasn't forgot what to do. She can talk that we don't have enough time but I'm going to make her see in a week not two that this is home and she needs to bring that ass right on back where she belongs.

"I haven't had no real dick in years so if you thought you could just stop because I won't bow down to your commands no longer then you are crazy for real, so take advantage like I am of the moment." She said coming up for air.

This was a side of her I don't ever recall seeing. This newfound independence was turning me on and with her sucking the shit out my dick I couldn't fight it no longer and I shot the biggest nut I have had in a long time down her throat and she gladly accepted every drop while swallowing it.

She crawled her way up and positioned herself on top of me while she slowly slid down on my dick, winding her hips as she came down to the base. She placed her feet flat on the bed, bending backwards a little bit, as she put her hands on my knees and began to bounce up and down. I had the perfect view, her natural size D tits bounced, and I could see my dick disappearing in and out of her pussy. I reached up with one hand and cuffed her left tit and took my other hand and put the right amount of pressure on her clitoris. That drove her crazy and she went down and stayed down so the base of my dick was met with her pussy and she began to just wind her hips, grinding her swollen clit on my finger and she came, came hard.

"I love you Damon, I'm cummin!"

"That's right baby cum all over your dick." I said as I seen my dick covered in her juices, even running down my balls. She climbed up off me, but I had yet to cum inside my soon to be wife. If I have to kidnap her and bring her to Jamaica with my son I'm doing it. Now that I heard her say she loves me and the way her pussy was gripping my dick there was no way she was walking away from me again.

I got up off the bed and grabbed Lynique pulling her by her hair, not in a way to hurt her but in a sexual pleasing way just so she was standing on the floor with me. I bent her over and slid back inside her, I wanted to punish her for taking that good pussy from me and leaving me to deal with all this mediocre pussy for the past 5 years. I lifted my leg and put it on the bed, so I could really go in deep. I was hitting her with short deadly strokes, no need to play nice anymore, I was chasing a nut and I wanted nothing more than to bust all up in her hoping that with her not being on birth control that I would give her a late Christmas gift. If I had to trap her by keeping her barefoot and pregnant then that's what I'm bout to do, shit bitches been doing it to men for years.

I was pounding the shit out her pussy, but she was taking it and was meeting me thrust for thrust, so I stopped with the short deep strokes and began to pull almost all the way out and quickly fill her back up with my dick. I could feel my stomach tightening so I knew I was about to nut and so did Lynique because she tried to move out the way, but I held onto her waist and released every bit I had in me and I stayed inside for a minute to make sure nothing escaped.

CHAPTER SIX

Lynique

Tomorrow is Christmas, well the one my brother was planning on having with me coming to town after the holidays had passed, and once again I am spending the night at Damon's house. I have yet to spend a night with my family, but we spent the days over there. Damon just wants to spend as much time with me and Jr as possible. We haven't had sex again but every night I'm in his bed, in his arms, getting the best sleep in the world. I missed this part of him, I keep telling myself not to get too comfortable because in a few more days I will be leaving and even though I know now we will need to have contact due to our son, it will be hard. He has turned his phone off, so all his female companions weren't interrupting us, and I was surprised when none came knocking on his door, but he shut those thoughts down telling me no one knew about this house, if he spent

115

a night with them it was back in the city.

We left Jr. yesterday for a few hours to go shopping for him, Damon wanted to set his room up and make it the room of his dreams. He even bought a ton of gifts for Jr to open on our fake holiday, which I still had to wrap for him. He will have everything he needs right here at his dad's house for future visits. Damon is still saying this is home now and we aren't leaving but I'm not caving in. I must admit his temper has been good but that also can be an act because he is trying to sucker me in.

"Lynique go ahead and take my car to the house. I have a few last-minute things to get before tomorrow and some stops to make but I will be at the house soon." Damon said to me. All I thought was *I bet you had some things to buy and places to go.* I know I have no right to be upset, because I was no longer his girl and I would be leaving soon so he had to line up his bitches again, but that don't mean it didn't bother me. I snatched the keys from his hand and stormed out my brother's house calling for Jr to come on.

"Aye slow it down woman. Don't snatch shit from me again, you understand me?" He spoke, and I thought welp here comes the beast. I needed that reminder of what lives inside of him, but I didn't want to feel the full wrath of it nor did I want our son to know and see that side of his father. I didn't bother to respond, I just buckled my son in the car and got in and closed the door. I adjusted the seat and then it hit me, how would he get to his house if I had his car?

I beeped the horn and he came to the driver's side window.

"How you getting to your house if I'm taking your car? Why don't I just take mine and you can have yours.?"

"You ain't running away. Take my car, your brother is driving me."

"So, you going to make my brother drive you all around doing whatever when he has a whole event to set up for tomorrow and his family to be with, when I have a perfectly safe car right there." I said pointing towards my 2016 Honda Accord that was parked where I left it a few days ago, when I first arrived.

"Just go ahead, I'm not going to be long at all you will see. Just be ready for when I get back. Have a movie picked out for us and get those pajama sets ready for us to put on and have family night."

Damon had got us all onesie pajamas even himself one. Granted his was Polo but still I couldn't wait to capture him in his. I just started his car by hitting the start button and headed for 93 south to hit the highway. I must admit, his new home, located in the historic town of Newport RI was impressive. It took me about an hour to get to the house. I told Jr to get into a bath while I went and ordered some food. Just shortly after the food came, Damon walked in with nothing in his hands which only solidified my original thought, he wasn't out making moves, he was out with his hoes. They didn't have to worry because I'll be gone in a few days and they can have him back, it did feel good to know I can shut it all down whenever I came around. What he didn't know was I wasn't that far from him, I was closer to him than both of us was to the city.

Once we ate dinner, I went to shower and get into my pajamas and Damon did the same in the other bathroom, so Jr wouldn't ask us why was we in a shower together. We gathered back in the living room and put on Beauty and The Beast, the movie not the cartoon version. I popped us some popcorn and made us some crushed ice with Kool-Aid flavor on it like a slushy. Damon and I sat next to each other, I tucked my feet underneath my butt and our son was at Damon's feet on the floor where he wanted to sit. He never made it through the whole movie so while Damon carried him to his room, I cleaned up the cups and bowls then met him back in his room.

I pulled back the comforter and slid into the bed after placing my phone on the charger, so I had a full battery to record our son's face in the morning when he realized it was Christmas all over again but this time at his dad's house. When I looked over Damon was standing at the end of the bed now in his boxers.

"Lynique, here." He said handing me a manila envelope.

"What is it?" I asked.

"Just open it please."

Doing as he asked and curious as to what it could be I was surprised to see it was a deed to the house we were currently in now in my name.

"What is this for, I told you I had a home."

"And you will be selling it or rent it if you don't want to give it up, but I meant it this is your home, our sons home. Here are my keys to it, I will leave if you really want me to and go back to the city. But I want you and my son to be in the most secured and safe house possible and this is it."

"Right go back to the city to your whores you went to see, tonight right?"

"Actually, you're wrong. This is where I went." He said walking over to his jacket and pulled out a jewelry box.

"Lynique Andrews, will you please consider spending your life with me? I will do whatever you ask, anger management included. I don't want to lose you again."

Tears were falling, and I just couldn't answer him.

CHAPTER SEVEN

Lynique

I couldn't believe that I was given this house. I was confused about what I wanted to do. I mean realistically it is a better more secure home in a better location, not to mention the school system is much better than where I have been living. I do suppose I could earn an extra income and rent out the much smaller house I owned. I know Jr will love to move because he was complaining already about having to go back to a smaller room, and he couldn't wait to come visit in the summer and go swimming in the pool, but I still ain't sure I should do this. I don't want Damon to get it in his head he can control me. I mean yes, he gave me paperwork to the house that is now in my name, along with his key but then turned around and asked me to marry him. I didn't answer him, nor accept the ring because all my fears came rushing back to me,

119

I left for a good reason, I kept telling myself. Just because a week has passed and I haven't had his foot up my ass doesn't mean that he is a changed man and won't snap on me once I agree.

"What if I don't want this big of a house?" I asked him.

"Do you know how dumb you sound right now Lynique?" he said looking defeated.

"Probably as dumb as I looked for being your punching bag all those nights. We have had a wonderful week, we share a beautiful son, who I am and will forever be thankful for you giving me, but I still think about all the bad stuff too." I said now sitting fully up in the bed.

"I understand what you are saying, I do, but how else will I be able to show you that this time it will be different if you don't take the chance? I know you love me still, besides when you said it the other night, I feel it Lynique, I can see it in your eyes. Don't you think you are torturing yourself by denying what it is you really want, and that is us." He said.

Damon was making a lot of valid points and I just needed to think. I didn't want to make any quick decisions that I would later regret, after all it would defeat the purpose of me running in the first place. I have my son and his innocence to take into consideration a whole lot more than what I wanted for myself.

"After tomorrow, I need for you to go stay wherever it is you had in mind for you to stay and give me some space. You being here with me is clouding my judgement. I need to make up my mind and do what is best for everyone, but us acting like we are a happy family when it can just be a temporary feeling won't help us in the long run. I don't want to feel trapped, pushed nor forced into a situation again." I told him.

"Okay, I'm going to put this ring right here, in this top dresser drawer. When you, or if you decide to accept my proposal, I want you to walk to this drawer." He said as he opened it, and placed the box with the ring and his key inside and closed it, "take the ring and key out, slide it on your finger and come to me and hand me the key and I will be all yours, but until then Lynique you can't get upset if you see or hear about me with any other woman because we aren't together, as you wish."

Hearing Damon talk about giving his time and dick to another after spending the past week with him really bothered me but I knew I had no right to be mad.

"But you didn't have to just add that bit of information. You will be away from here and me so what you would be doing I would have no way to know, just like the past 5 years I didn't know every detail of what you been up to."

"Oh, but you wrong about that Lynique. I will go stay at my condo in the city but being away from you, I didn't agree to that. I will be here at least one night out the weekend spending time with my son, unless of course you are going to let me bring him to my spot."

"That's a no. He's just getting to know you, he won't be around your hoes. It's bad enough he had to see his mother fighting one of them the same day he met his father because the bitch didn't know her place nor how to watch her mouth."

"She did have some valid points, but I will never let anyone disrespect you." He said as he walked towards me after closing the drawer.

"What point did she have? That I should have sucked up the blows, deal with being hit for no reason at all? I'm worth more and I had a life inside of me I needed to protect. Her opinion nor anyone else's will ever matter to me. I did what I felt was needed to make sure I had a healthy pregnancy and safe childbirth." I informed him.

"I don't want to argue with you Lynique. Can we agree to disagree? I'm trying to work with you and do this your way. I'd cancel everyone right now, change my number and marry you tomorrow if you agreed to it. It's you that ain't hearing nor believing me so until you become mine again, I have needs to be met and they will be willing to stop, drop and roll for me. It's not like you will be around the corner for me to do a late night quick stop so someone going to have to service the beast." Damon said as he was now sitting at my feet on the bed.

"Man move!" I said now frustrated, I ain't want to hear or imagine him doing all that, and I was already vocal about it but he still carried on. Some things were better left unsaid and that was one of them. I knew I will be laying in bed every night picturing him giving that good dick away to someone else. I know Damon has a high sex drive and can't get enough so I knew 9/10 he will be with someone every night of the week who wasn't me satisfying them, while I laid in bed alone back to playing with myself.

CHAPTER EIGHT

Damon

Lynique thought by telling me to move that she was going to be able to throw a silent tantrum and go to sleep but I had something else planned. I was going to remind her until I did leave to go stay at the condo in the city what she was in so many words allowing me to give to others. I was going to give her the best dick down in history tonight. I am relieved my son, once knocked out would sleep through an atomic bomb going off in his room so he won't be waking up to his mother's screams. She keeps bringing up how I put my hands on her in the past, and yes, I was wrong for that, so instead I was planning on punishing her with this deadly weapon that hung low.

When I didn't move right away like she demanded, she tried to kick me off, but I grabbed ahold of her left foot as she was laying on her right side, and then I took her right foot in my other hand and spread her legs. I just looked at her pussy print in the thin fabric of her panties. I leaned down and just blew at a close range on her pussy and felt her tense up, as she let out a slight moan.

"Tell me what you want me to do to you right now baby?" I said to her.

"Just do what you do baby, you know how to drive me crazy." She stuttered, as I put my mouth on the outside of her panties but covered her pearl and blew hard, letting the heat from my mouth send sensations to her, I could feel the heat radiating back from her pussy.

I let her feet go, but Lynique kept her legs spread wider than an eagle flying high above, and I planned on taking her head to a higher level than that. I took my thumb and applied just enough pressure above her clitoris while I slid the lacey material to the side, my finger gliding up and down the opening of her pussy. You see, Lynique's pussy had this power behind it that some investors could use to create the world's greatest vacuum cleaner because when my finger got to her opening it sucked my finger on in, and I went with it. As I was working my finger I gradually added another one inside then brought my face back down to her pussy. I bit lightly on her now swollen pearl. Lynique grabbed ahold of my head and pushed it into her pussy, holding it still as she grinded on my face. I was loving the way she was tasting as her pussy walls was gripping my fingers while I was stroking her with them. I removed my fingers and forced her hands from my head and stood up to remove my clothes. While I was doing that, Lynique moved her hand to her pussy and was rubbing her pussy inside of her panties, until I was close enough for her other hand to grab ahold of my dick that was standing straight at attention. She took her finger from out her pussy, and underwear and stuck it in her mouth savoring the taste of her own pussy making me jealous because I wanted to go back to enjoying the sweetness it held. I reached down and tore her tiny ass panties off that created a barrier, not wanting to take the time to have her lift up and remove them. I dove back head first to finish getting my favorite snack but this time

I wanted to try something new, to test her skills, that I knew she had but this was a position we never tried in the past and I wanted to see if she could handle sucking the dick while I ate her pussy at the same time. I stopped eating her pussy and moved her from my dick, as hard as it was but it was only going to be for a few seconds. I reached for her and lifted her off the bed but placed us in the 69 position while I was standing. Her pussy was calling for me, so I went back to licking and sucking on it as she once again wrapped her hands and then mouth on my dick. I guess she was loving the way I was eating her pussy as she began to wind her hips almost causing me to drop her.

I backed my mouth from her pussy and told her watch out, so she could stop sucking my dick upside down, now thinking shit what if all her blood rushes to her head, but baby was in a zone and was going to town and I felt my knees getting weak from the sensation she was bringing to my body. Turning around where I could now fall back on the bed, I did just that then went back to eating her pussy, but this time it took nothing for her to cum and I sucked it all up.

Don't ask me where Lynique learned the next position but it was like she got into a crab position as she stopped sucking my dick but crawled to where she positioned her pussy at the tip and eased her way down, head still bent as I felt the tip of her tongue at the base of my dick, she then grabbed my balls and popped one in her mouth. I never knew she was so flexible and could bend her body in the manner to do the impossible, had I known this I would have chased her ass down 5 years ago, when she ran off on me. It took me no longer than 4 minutes to release deep in her in this position.

CHAPTER NINE

Lynique

I know what Damon thought he was doing, but I had to switched it up on him. You see I been doing yoga since Jr was two months old and I was cleared by the doctors, that and when you must resort to watching porn so much you learn a whole lot. Once I felt his dick pulsating inside of me knowing he just dropped a huge amount of cum in me I knew I had to make a mental note to head to the doctors soon for birth control. I don't care what he was just telling me about once a week coming here for our son, we both knew he would be in my bed on those days and I'm going to need to get on something, that is if I wasn't already pregnant, not from tonight but from my first night back in town.

I untucked my head from the position it was in and I used my stomach muscle strength to flip my body over to where I had my body in a half handstand on the floor, my pussy open and with an easy accessible entry. I dreamed of trying this position for years and it was about to happen. I just prayed that I was strong enough to hold myself steady, but I was about to find out.

"Damn, baby what have you been studying lately, got you doing these flips and flops and landing in these positions, even I couldn't come up with. I'm about to beat this shit up like this here." Damon said while biting his bottom lip, and without warning or even going slowly he pushed all the way in and began giving me steady strokes, evenly timed and paced, but each one hitting my spot. I was fighting to hold on, but it was useless. After a dozen or so times of him hitting my weak spot I did something I haven't done in years, I squirted and due to the position, I was in it was landing on my stomach, but he didn't stop, and I couldn't take it.

"Baby, wait, I'm weak and I have to move." I said trying to regain strength because that orgasm took a lot from me.

"Nope, hold on baby, you think you can introduce me to a new position and because you busted already you can just change positions, you have to stay still let me have some fun." He said while continuously beating up my pussy.

"Bae, you have too much stamina for me to stay like this without causing my body to have Charlie horses and a migraine later, hit it from behind." I begged him, but it fell on deaf ears.

I felt another strong orgasm coming on and my body was shaking but he wasn't letting up. "Damon, baby please oh my god I can't take it baby. I'm bout to cum again, fuck baby I can't do this, I can't allow you to give my dick to anyone else. I love you I'll marry you, don't leave."

I didn't know if I really felt what I was saying or even wanted it but the way he had my body convulsing back to back to back, I was liable to admit to doing sins I never have.

"You ready for this bitch?" he hollered out as I felt his movements speed up knowing he was about to bust another one.

"Fuck me baby, give me that shit, shoot all that shit in your pussy baby, I'm about to cum right along with you again." I screamed out.

Damon slid out of me and I barely made it fully on the bed when he stopped me from laying down, he placed his hands on my hips bringing them up, then pushed my head down, put a hand on the middle of my lower back applying pressure where he created the perfect arch. I ain't going to lie, as amazing as the 3 new positions I was put in tonight was, this will always be my favorite, it allowed him to bang the tip of his dick in a place not easily found within, like a double hole as he once described and when he was in that place it was a constant orgasm not multiple back to back. It was a feeling I desired for years to feel again and just thinking how I was about to feel it again had me dripping.

What I was really wanting was him to enter and go right to that hidden place but instead he slid in slow and not fully, only putting half of his dick in and then pulling all the way out and it was driving me crazy. He knew I wanted him to fuck me and he wanted to play games, when he entered me this time I quickly backed up so that he filled me up, when I did so my ass bounced, and Damon slapped it.

"You ain't slick, you better stay in your place Lynique or you won't get what you want, I'm not ready to go there right now, let me savor the feeling of just being in you for a minute." He said breathing heavy as he was moving in and out side to side slowly.

I let him remain doing that for about two minutes before I was tired of the anticipation building, wondering when was he going to really bless me so I ignored what he said and I began really backing it up on him to the point he was now just standing still straight up and letting me fuck him by backing up on his dick, but no matter how hard I tried to get it so he entered that place I couldn't and he knew it.

"As amusing as this is and I want you to suffer baby I can't fight the urge anymore, daddy is bout to go home." He said while putting one foot up on the bed and gripping my hips tight.

At first when he said that I thought he was talking about stopping all together and going home without us making it 3 for the count for him, but once I seen that foot on the bed I already knew what he was about to do and what home he was about to visit.

"You ready? Remember you asked for it." he warned me.

Maybe I had forgot how before it got to feeling good, it was painful, but a good pain, but it still hurt nonetheless. It felt like he was rearranging my uterus when he would ram in and out of me and then POP he was in there, in that deep hole within me, and he just stopped and began to just wind his hips while being so deep inside me. I was like a faucet a child left on by accident, it was a never-ending feeling that was indescribable.

"Lynique keep cummin baby, just feeling my dick swimming in this hole filled with your warm cum is making me about to nut." He said

It didn't take long for him to release again and just fall on top of me, with his dick deep embedded in me. I collapsed on the bed and by doing so it caused him to fall from my magic spot, but he remained inside of me for a few minutes.

CHAPTER TEN

Damon

The next morning, I was still floating. You would think after all that we would have knocked out, nope instead we went for another round in the shower then again when we got in the bed.

I was trying to get out the bed, so I could make Lynique breakfast in bed before we had to get up and head to wake Jr up then head to her brother's house, but she felt me remove my arm from around her and she stretched.

"Where you going?" she asked groggily.

"I was going to make your nosey ass breakfast as a surprise and a thank you, but you spoiled it."

"Stay in bed, don't move and bring the cold air in, keep me

warm." She said reaching to pull me back towards her. I allowed her to and she put her head back on my chest.

After a few minutes of a comfortable silence she spoke up, "Last night was amazing Damon, thank you. But I kind of made some promises I'm not so sure was the right ones to make under the circumstances."

I knew just what she was getting at and while I didn't take what she said in the heat of the moment as her word I was going to use it against her.

"Maybe if I opened up and shed some light on my childhood, something I never did before you will understand just a little bit why I was so bad to you. It wasn't you, it was me. I wasn't taught to respect a woman, nor how to love one. My father beat on my step mother and she in turn use to fuck with me and I'm not talking about hitting on me. She did things to me that wasn't appropriate."

"Are you telling me you were sexually abused by your step mother?" she asked while lifting her head to look at me with shock on her face.

"Yes, and I hated her and every other woman for it. I always said to myself if my own mother could abandon me, my step mother abuse me then how was it possible for you to love me the way you would say. I've always loved you Lynique, but I thought by controlling you and hitting on you was a form of showing love and I'm sorry for that. I see now that I wasn't showing you love, I was hurting the only woman who loved me."

"Why wouldn't you ever share this with me in the past Damon? I wouldn't have looked at you fucked up, I would have gone to therapy with you to help you let it go and not have ran off."

"About that, thank you for leaving me." I told her even taking

132

myself by surprise.

"Huh?" she asked confused.

"Had you not left, I don't know for certain I wouldn't have had a moment and risked Jr being born by putting my hands on you, had you not taken off and me running around with all these dumb ass women I wouldn't have learned to miss you, to appreciate what I had. You did what you had to for you and our son and for that I thank you, and now I'm realizing that you taught me a valuable lesson and I won't make those same mistakes I made years ago. I want to cherish you and love you and treat you the way you deserve to be. I want to shower you with the world and make it so you never have to worry about anything ever again, not even me hurting you physically or mentally."

"Where do we go from here?" she asked with her voice cracking.

"We build and we fix what I broke, but I need you to do it. I can't do it alone. If you want to take back what you said while I was in your guts last night then I understand, and I give you my word, I will still cut the hoes off and go to the condo and let you have your space, but only if you work with me to fix our family. Put that ring on your finger Lynique and give me something to work hard for and fight my demons." I told her.

"Baby you ain't going to the city, you are staying here with me and Jr. Yes, I screamed that out because you were tearing the pussy up, as always, but only way to know if we going to make it is to jump in with both feet. But Damon, listen to me, I'm serious, if you have one slip up and even grab me with force I'm done." She warned me.

"No, revise that. I'll be grabbing you with force every night, as I hit you with those long deep strokes." I told her as my dick got hard.

"Daddy, Mommy is it time for me to have my second Christmas

yet?' Jr said while walking into the bedroom, where I had left the door unlocked. I'm going to have to make sure that I start locking that bitch at night because I was just about to climb on top of his mother and make sure I planted another baby inside.

"Yes son, go on and brush your teeth and me and your mother will be right down stairs, so you can open them."

I got up and walked to the top drawer to grab some boxers and while I was in the drawer I grabbed the ring to go put it on her finger.

"Will you marry me Lynique?" I asked her again before sliding it on her finger."

"Yes, and I think I have the perfect date set already." She said while admiring the ring.

"What's that?"

"Feb. 14th "she replied.

"Sounds good to me, that gives us under two months to get everything set up." I said as I leaned over and kissed her.

Hand in hand we walked down the stairs where our overly excited son was waiting for us.

CHAPTER ELEVEN

Lynique

Wedding Day

I couldn't believe it; the past 6 weeks have been nothing short of amazing. I am now married to my son's father. I honestly didn't see it happening when I got in my car and took that dreadful ride to Boston to see my family and introduce everyone to Jr.

Me and Damon was on the floor dancing to our first dance as husband and wife. I had my head rested on his chest as we swayed side to side. I knew now was the perfect time to give him the news I had just found out myself.

"Husband?" I said lifting my head up to look him in the eyes. I loved saying it and been calling him that all night.

"Yes, my beautiful wife?" he replied.

"We have another date to add to a list of them to remember?"

"Who can forget A Valentine's Day wedding date?" he said laughing.

"Not that date."

"Then what date, your birthday, Jr's birthday?" he asked me.

"No before Halloween comes we will have a date to remember."

"Okay you lost me baby." He said.

"We are pregnant." I told him.

Damon stopped dancing, looked at me to see if I was joking and when he seen I was serious he yelled out, "That's what I'm talking bout. A nigga got a new baby on the way."

Everyone watching us while we had our first dance broke out in applause.

"Baby, don't run this time." He said.

"Only direction I'm running is to you." I said as the song ended and we walked off the dance floor.

"You have no choice in the matter now Lynique! You belong to me officially." Damon said, and it made the hairs on the back of my neck stand. I'm not sure why. Everything has been all love and peace since I been back. I quickly said a silent prayer that I was just paranoid, and things would remain as great as they have been. Deciding that it will be best to not respond I wrapped my arms around his neck and gave him a kiss in which he reciprocated.

"I can't believe we are married, when I was giving birth to Jr. I cried, not from the pain but because I was a single mother with a new baby boy. I was alone, and all I could think was how was I going to raise him to be a strong man?"

"Whose fault is that Lynique? Huh? This time you won't be alone. I will be right there, camera all up in your pussy watching my baby enter the world. We ain't going to keep bringing up you leaving with my son either, you understand me?" Damon said, then kissed me on the cheek, walking off.

I smiled while looking around making sure no-one seen the tension between me and my new husband. Seeing that everyone was enjoying themselves, I walked to the table set up for me and Damon, taking a seat. I was lost in my thoughts, its not like I regret marrying my sons father, I just kept getting this nagging feeling within that things were going to change now that we made it legal. However, this time I was prepared to defend myself and before he could hurt me, I will hurt him.

Just the fact I had these kinds of thoughts running thru my mind on my wedding day was wrong, I felt a lone tear fall down my face and before I could wipe it away I heard Damon clear his throat.

"Why are you sitting over here looking like you lost your best friend and crying on our wedding day Lynique?"

"It's hormones Damon. What makes you think that I'm thinking bad things, maybe I'm in shock. I am your wife now. I married my one and only love. Perhaps this tear is a drop of happiness." I replied while wiping my cheek before it left a streak in my makeup.

"Yeah okay, I hope that is what it was for. I been trying to get your attention for the past 5 minutes, it's time to cut the cake so come on."

I got up and rounded the table. Damon looked at me sideways

with a confused look on his face before he snatched my hand and led me to the other side of the room where our 5 layered cake was on a table. It was covered in edible flowers in the colors of silver and royal blue. We posed for the photographers. Damon stood behind me with his arms reaching around me, hands on mine while I held the knife and together we cut into the bottom layer. The bottom layer was my favorite of all the ones we tested 2 weeks ago. It was a chocolate chip cake with chocolate ganache filling. Once the cake was sliced we used the cake server to pull the piece apart from the rest and placed it on a small glass plate. I picked up a fork and fed a small piece to Damon, he wanted our first slice to be a different flavor, but I got what I wanted. He then took the fork and fed me a slice as our guest broke out clapping and hollering.

The waitstaff took the cake to the kitchen area to cut it into slices for everyone to have a piece. Me and Damon went to get a few dances in with a small crowd that was getting down on the floor to Kendrick Lamar's All The Stars feat. SZA. The song went off and I went to go see what Jr was doing. He was having a blast with his cousins. I'm still not use to having to share his attention with anyone. It's been just the two of us for so long that the fact he be off paying me no mind lowkey hurt. I walked up, bent down and gave him a kiss on the cheek.

"Awe Ma why you have to do that?" he said wiping my kiss off.

"You never had a problem with my kisses before baby, what has changed?" I inquired.

"I'm not a little boy anymore. You're embarrassing me." he whispered while looking at the little kids standing and watching us.

"Well excuse me." I stood straight back up, feeling a little hurt and went to walk off.

"Ma, wait! I'm sorry. I love you too, just don't kiss me anymore okay?" Jr said with a smirk on his face looking just like his daddy.

"You got it." I winked at him and walked back over to where all the adults were having a good time, drinking and dancing.

CHAPTER TWELVE

Damon

I couldn't wait til this reception was over, so I could go home, change and head to a surprise honeymoon I had planned last minute for me and Lynique. I made arrangements with Tino, her brother to stay with Jr for the 5 days we were gone, and I know that Lynique is going to have an issue with it. She was very protective of our son, and that is a good thing, but was no way I wanted a 5 year old cock blocking on my honeymoon, son or not.

As the last few guests were saying goodbye, preparing to leave I looked around the ballroom and couldn't find Lynique. I knew if she didn't get the opportunity to say goodbye to Jr before Tino and his family left to go home.

"Aye have you seen my wife?" I asked one of the servers that was cleaning up empty glasses from tables.

"I'm not sure who is your wife?" he responded sarcastically.

"Gee, perhaps the fucking bride!" I barked.

"Damn, you just got her, and she ran away from you already. My condolences." he laughed then turned his back to me to walk towards the kitchen with the big gray container filled with dirty glasses and empty beer bottles.

His slick mouth just landed him in a beatdown. I looked across the room and yelled for Tino to have his wife Meeka to take the kids outside to his car. He knew by me saying that, that shit was bout to pop off. Once the kids was out of sight, I lightly jogged to catch up with this bitch and tapped him on the shoulder.

"Aye, say that shit again for me my dude." I said giving him that I dare you.

"Why is you bothering me, you see I'm trying to fucking work so these hoe ass niggas can get they foot off my neck. So, your bitch ran off on you, she probably being dicked down in a bathroom somewhere, take it up with her not me partner."

"One, two, three."

"Nigga is you counting?" Tino asked me when he finally made his way to where I was about to lay this fool out. He is taking this tux I was wearing like I'm not about to bring that hood nigga out and fuck his entire life up. He wasn't gonna have to worry bout having papers on him or the law with they foot on his neck as he referred because I was getting ready to break that shit.

WHAM!

I knocked the fuck out noodle legs. As soon as my fist met his fucking jaw his legs became soft and he dropped to his knees.

"Now come again? What was you saying about my wife busy being fucked in a bathroom?" I yelled as I brought my leg up and kicked his ass in the chest, now making him fall over. Before he could fix his mouth to say anything, I lifted my leg and kicked him one more time.

"ARGH!" he yelled.

"Oh, you ain't so tough now are you little bitch." I said as I was getting ready to steal on him again before I heard Lynique yell out.

"Stop Damon. What the fuck is wrong with you?" she asked.

"Where the fuck was you at?" now amped the hell up, having images of my new wife bent over some dirty public restroom getting fucked by a stranger with my baby inside of her.

"Matter of fact, don't answer that yet, let's fucking go NOW!" I yelled the last part and my voice echoed through the room. Just moments ago, it was a joyous evening and I was seeing red now.

"Bruh, you need to calm all that down. Don't do your wife, my sister like that. Remember what happened the last time you scared her?" Tino stated.

"I dare her to take off again pregnant and rob me of seeing this baby be born. I'll be a single father when it's all over and done with, I promise you that."

"Tino, will you bring me to your house tonight? My husband clearly is losing his damn mind and brought back the real Damon." Lynique said.

"Bruh go on with your family and take care of my son. We will be back in a few days. She's good, I ain't gonna hurt her." I told

142

him looking him in the eye like a man, so he knew I was being real.

"Aight bruh. Save travels, Lynique relax. Love you sis." he said then turned to head out.

"Sir, what happened in here?" the manager to the hotel we rented the ballroom at asked me.

"Man, his shoes must be too big or something, he tripped and fell carrying that big ass tray of shit." I said as I grabbed Lynique's hand, so we could get the fuck out of there before these people called the cops and I spent my wedding night in a jail cell.

Entering the car, Lynique got in full of attitude but I had something in mind for that shit. I was about to knock that shit out of her as soon as we got to Antigua. I wanted to stop at the house and change clothes. I already had our bags packed and placed in the trunk, so I opted to head to the airstrip before her little ass tried to escape.

"Bring me to get my son then home!" Lynique demanded.

"Did you enjoy your special day baby?" I asked her, toying with her. I knew she was mad but ask me if I gave a fuck. I still didn't know where the hell her ass had disappeared too causing me to beat that boy's ass at the hotel.

"So, you're just going to kidnap me now?"

"You belong to me, we are married. I ain't doing anything illegal."

"You are taking me against my will, that is kidnapping, married or not."

"Will you please just be quiet Lynique, dammit."

"Bring me the fuck to my son NOW!" she screamed.

I looked over at her as I put the car in park, we were now at the airstrip and the private jet was ready for us to depart. I laughed at her, got out the car, grabbed the suitcases and handed them to the stewardess then returned to get my hard-headed wife.

"Lynique get out the car and let's go."

"I told you I am not going anywhere with you where you can hurt me."

"I ain't going to hurt you, punish you, yes but I will not hurt you now come on these people are waiting."

"I didn't get to say bye to my son, and who knows what you going to do to me wherever this plane lands. I need for him to know I love you."

"Will you bring your dumb ass on or I'm going to drag your ass on that plane."

"Drag me then."

With that I reached in between and unhooked the seatbelt. I put my right arm under her legs, grabbed her right arm and put it around my neck. With my left arm around her waist I pulled her from the car and carried her bridal style to the steps of the plane. One by one I walked up just looking her in her eyes daring her to kick and fight and giving these people a reason to be suspicious of me really kidnapping my wife.

CHAPTER THIRTEEN

Lynique

I didn't realize how tired I was until I felt Damon nudging me to let me know we had landed and to get up. I wanted to sleep longer but I knew I wouldn't be able to on the plane, yet I didn't really want to get off it. I wasn't sure was it safe too, and what Damon may have planned. I saw that look in his eye when I walked in from using the bathroom and he was standing over that waiter. I'm not sure what caused him to beat that man up but when he looked up at me, I knew it was over me. I never saw the man laying on the floor with his hands up to block the rain of blows Damon was about to land.

"I don't want to move; can't I just finish sleeping first?" I asked.

"No Lynique you can't sleep on the plane, plus you are pregnant, you need to be thinking about the baby. Don't you think the bed that awaits you will be better than that seat?" he asked me.

"Perhaps you're right."

I stood up, stretched then looked around for my purse. This time around if Damon thought he would put his hands on me I would be prepared. In my purse I kept a variety of items to keep me safe, from mace to a box cutter. I even had a blow torch type lighter with some spray to light his ass up. Seeing that it had slipped onto the floor, I bent down to pick it up which gave Damon the opportunity to smack my ass real hard. In recent times with how amazing things between us has been I would not have flinched, it would have turned me on but not right now. The images are still fresh in my mind about what happened at our reception.

Dragging my feet to the car that was waiting on the tarmac, a man in a suit was standing at the rear door waiting to open it for us.

"Woman will you pick up the speed, by the time I get your ass to the room it will be time to board that plane and go home." Damon said.

Muttering under my breath I stated, "That don't sound like a bad thing." this trip must only be a day long then if he is talking like that. Not wanting to anger him, I picked up my speed and walked faster. I may as well get whatever he had planned for me over with.

I never bothered to ask where he was bringing me, and like I mentioned I knocked out right away on the flight over, so looking out the window of the black on black Tahoe with tinted windows so no one could see in, I was in awe at the site of a beautiful shoreline. Living in Massachusetts and being on the water of the Atlantic Ocean you would think seeing beaches wouldn't phase me. However, our beaches didn't look remotely close to what I was seeing as we drove along. Our beaches weren't picture perfect, something you could entice visitors to come lay on and swim. I knew we had to have been on an Island, which Island was still a mystery to me.

Arriving to the resort Damon had reserved for us, I was speechless it was beyond anything I had ever imagined staying in. Damon checked us in and we were lead to a Deluxe room, on ground level. Right outside the double doors on the other side of our suite was the beach, I am talking steps away. The scene pulled me in making me not stop even to place my purse down, nor paying attention to what Damon was doing with the bellhop. As tired as I was just an hour ago, I was now wide awake. I wanted to take my shoes off and feel that crystal white sand on my feet. I slid open the floor to ceiling door and stepped out, taking a deep breath, soaking in the fresh smell of the ocean.

"It's almost as beautiful as you Lynique." Damon spoke as he walked up behind me. He wrapped his arms around me and I laid my head on him. Everything I felt since leaving the reception faded in this very moment.

"I really don't want to bring it up, but I have to, and it may as well be now. What the hell happened back at the hotel when I went to the bathroom Damon? What could that man have done so bad for you to put your hands on him, on our wedding night?"

"I asked if he saw you, he talked shit, even went as far as telling me you were getting your back blown out in the bathroom, so I hit his ass and I'd do it again. So, you was in the bathroom, I see. With who and why is the question." he responded.

Pulling away and turning to him, I said "Are you really asking me that dumb question? I just vowed to fucking love you, spend my life with you and even when I wasn't with you for all those years, I belonged to only you so don't you fucking dare insinuate that I was doing anything wrong. I had to fucking piss okay. Do you know how hard it is to piss in a dress with layers of material? Move so I can actually get the fuck out of this bitch." I said pushing away from him. I wanted this gown off hours ago but seeing as he wanted to jump on a plane I never got to change out of it.

"I'm sorry Lynique, its just when it comes to you I lose it. The thought of anyone having what belongs to me drives me insane. Let me help you out that shit." Damon said walking in the room with me. I could see what he had in mind to do once it was off, sadly for him it wasn't happening. I didn't care that this was our honeymoon, I was pissed off.

CHAPTER FOURTEEN

Damon

Today is day three of our honeymoon. Lynique has not given me any love, she complains she is tired but has had tons of energy to go do different tourist things and shop. Every time I go near her to touch her she flinches and it's pissing me off. I know I had a problem with my hands in the past but I thought all was forgiven and was put behind us. Why now, why after we got married? I do know that when she brings that pretty ass in from the beach, I'm getting me some of that pussy, she has no choice in the matter. In the meantime I decided to power up my work phone and check on things and make sure everything back home was going good. Before it was fully up and running the notifications was going crazy. I had over 150 texts messages from different top workers of mine, including some from Tino. He never used my private number to discuss business and when I was on the phone with my son this morning Tino gave no inclination that he needed to holla at me regarding work. I decided to call him first and see what the hell was going on.

"Yo, talk to me." I said as soon as he answered.

"Man, ain't no simple way of saying this and you know I ain't bout to dance around the topic but what's good with this last shipment? The shit is stepped on more than a college courtyard during a stomp the yard event." he told me.

"What you mean? Nothing has changed in my supplier. It's been the same shit for years. Let me get at my pops and see what the fuck is going on, I'll get back at you. Get ahold of everyone else. Tell em I'm on it and close down shit til I hit the pavement."

"Say no more, I'll see you in a few days when you touch down." Tino said.

"I'm not sure if I'm coming right back, it all depends on how this phone call with my father goes, but I'll be in touch. Lynique will be back tho." I said hanging up the phone quickly because I seen my wife walking towards the sliding door and I didn't want to set her off with me taking care of business.

"Who was you talking to that you had to click real fast?" she asked coming in questioning me like I already knew she would.

"Man, go on with that shit. Go get in a shower, I want to taste some pussy and salt water and sand are not a special ingredient I want in my mouth."

"Answer the question Damon?" with her hand on her hip she stood her ground.

"Your damn brother, now go do what I asked you to do. This

150

our honeymoon and you have yet to give me my pussy."

"I was going to wash regardless, I'll decide if I'm going to let you taste it while I'm in there."

Oh yeah, her little ass was bout to be punished. Time for me to show her who the fuck is wearing the pants. She walked off in the direction of the bathroom and I walked outside so I could call my father and talk in private.

On the third ring he picked up.

"Pops what the fuck is up with this new batch of shit you sent over?"

"Oh, you no like it? Well I don't like hearing bout my son getting married and having a family and no tell me bout it. You bring my new family to meet me and we will talk in person bout the other shit." He demanded then hung up.

I never wanted Lynique to meet them people let alone my son. I had a major decision to make but right now I needed to head back inside and to that bathroom to show my wife who the fuck is really the boss. As I was heading towards the bathroom I was stripping out my clothes piece by piece so once I opened that glass shower door, she would know just what I was there for.

All I had to do was glance at her body and my dick sprang to life. I stepped all the way in and closed the door. I grabbed her by her hair and pulled her head back. My mouth found it's way to her neck and I bit down on it. A moan escaped her mouth and her body relaxed at the same time my dick was jumping. I ain't want to waste time with foreplay I needed to hurry and feel the warmth of her pussy around my dick. I guess she needed to feel my dick in her just as bad, although she was playing games the last few days because after about 15 strokes she had my shit glistening with her juices. She came once and I could tell she was ready to release again just that fast. Remembering I wanted to punish her for holding out and having an attitude the past few days I pulled out before she could bust again. I smacked her hard as hell on her ass, while I still had my hand wrapped in her hair and I pulled it back again, with force.

'Ouch, what the fuck is wrong with you?" she yelled.

"Shut the fuck up, you withheld my pussy from me, I'm going to show you what happens when you do that. A nigga got blue balls, you going to have a black and blue ass."

"But that hurts!" she voiced.

"That is the purpose, my nuts been hurting for 3 days watching you walk around half naked on a beach, but you didn't care. You were in your feelings over me fucking a nigga up for saying some shit bout you."

"No, it was what you said to me and how you looked at me."

"Lynique please just shut up, let me get a nut off, damn my dick bout to go soft."

"Then let me get it hard again."

"Nah, I want to straight fuck, no foreplay just me in your guts is what I want, so bend the hell over."

"I can't you got my head pulled back."

"that got nothing to do with your body, bend the hell over." I told her as I helped her. I did however ease up on her hair. She is still my wife and the woman I love who has my baby inside of her, so I needed to ease up I realized. She wasn't no hoe in the street.

I re-entered her and this time I took my time, she thru her ass back at me while I was gliding in and out from the back. It didn't take long for me to explode in her. I grabbed the wash cloth and lathered it up with soap and washed her back before turning her around and while kissing her I was washing the front of her body. Once we were both clean we stepped out and went to the bed. I didn't know how I was going to tell her that she would be flying back to the states alone while I went to Jamaica. She been acting like a real moody bitch, so I was sure it would set her off.

CHAPTER FIFTEEN

Lynique

"What the fuck you mean you catching a flight to Jamaica? You ain't coming home with me to be with your son. We haven't seen him in 5 days." I stood looking at Damon infuriated with him. He just told me he had to go take care of business in Jamaica before he headed home with me. Like who the hell does shit like that.

"It wasn't my plan, but in my line of work, as you know things happen and this needs to be addressed immediately. Had we not been on our honeymoon I would have already been over there dealing with my father."

"So why can't we all go, let's go get Jr and go on a family trip." I asked him.

154

"Because I don't ever want you meeting them people. I told you what my childhood was like and I will do whatever I have to do to protect you and my kids so by saying that, no I'm not making a family trip and bringing you and Jr. If you want us to go on a family trip we can when I get back home."

"When will that be exactly?"

"I can't say for sure, but as soon as I possibly can get back to your pretty ass I will."

"Damon, we are about to have our second child. You have enough money; don't you think it's time to give up your position? You don't do anything anyway."

"Oh, I don't? Do you think the money you spend magically appears in the account, I may not have to be out all night or in the streets even Lynique but that don't mean I don't work."

"Mmm whatever you say. I'll see you when you get back, maybe." I was really feeling so kind of way. I loved Damon, but I miss the life I built over the years I was gone. If he doesn't figure out what is more important and put his family first, then I was leaving again.

"Don't get the fact we married fucked up baby, the next time you run, I will hunt you down and kill you." he leaned in and gave me a kiss before he got out the car to open my door, so I could board the plane back to the states.

"See talking like that makes me want to leave."

"Look relax baby. I'm going to try to set something up for your brother to pick up work from someone else and I'm going to tell my pops I'm not doing this anymore. Happy now!"

"I am, but it's only for our future and the safety of our family. I'll get a job if you think we will need money Damon. I just don't want to lose you to be it by death or you going to jail. The life was all fun and games before we got married and have 2 kids to worry about."

"You ain't getting a job okay like you said I have enough damn money. That was an insult. Look just get on the damn plane Lynique and I'll see you in a day or two, standing here throwing a temper tantrum like you are our sons age ain't getting me to go do what I have to do any faster."

The next day

"Tino, what do you mean he ain't answering either phone for you? He ain't picking up for me or you. I'm coming to your house. I'm going crazy sitting here not knowing what is going on." I stated before hanging up the phone. I wasn't about to give my brother the chance to talk me into staying in my house.

I put some clothes on Jr and headed out in a snowstorm to go to the city. I wasn't paying attention as I went through a light and a school bus rammed into my car spinning it before I crashed into a tree. I heard Jr screaming as things turned black.

CHAPTER SIXTEEN

Damon

"What do you mean they are both hurt and in the hospital?" I roared into the phone as Tino told me that Lynique and Jr was in a bad accident and was in the hospital.

"She was frantic on the phone, wanting to know what you were doing and why you haven't called. You told me to keep her in the dark about what was going on, so I told her you didn't call me. She was on her way here to my house to use my phone I am assuming. Next thing I knew the hospital had called me to tell they was in a bad accident. I'm on my way to the hospital but I thought I'd call you while I was on my way there." he said.

"Fuck, hurry up and get there, I'm wrapping up this shit and I'll be on the first thing out this bitch. Tell my wife I love her."

"Of course, I am already on my way to the hospital, breaking

157

laws on the way. You know that's my little sister and I'm going to be make sure she is good."

"That's automatic." I hung up the phone and turned around to face my father.

"Like I was saying before you so ignorantly took that phone call, I want to meet my new family members, once that happens then I will send the proper product to you." my father said.

"You can keep your product, keep it all. I came to tell you in person that I am done. I have a family to think about. My wife wants me out so I'm out."

"Son, you're talking dumb. You can't just decide when you can walk away, that ain't how it works, and you know that." he said laughing from behind his desk at me.

"I'm not going to be the kind of father you were. I'm going to lead my son to be a positive person. I almost never met my son, because I learned too many of your bad traits. It almost cost me my wife, she left because I put hands on her. My son will not be a product of that environment, as I was of yours."

"You ungrateful little motherfucker! I gave you a good life, you could have gone to live with that bitch of a mother in a shack instead of up here in the hills eating well and living good."

"I would have preferred it then have your wife put her hands on me and have her way with me." I spat.

"What are you saying Damon?"

"Just what I said, you a smart man, aren't you? Why you think I hate it here and couldn't wait to leave. You tossed my mother, whoever she is to the trash for a whore."

"Don't you speak on my wife that way. You may not make it home to yours." he said now getting visually upset.

"Go on do it, but I'm leaving here now and never looking back. My family needs me back home. Goodbye father."

"You're making a mistake."

"I just might be, only way to know for sure is to leap." I told him as I walked out his door. One thing I did know for certain, he may cut me off from providing product or even financially had I needed it for going against him and saying what I had to say about his sneaky wife but I was still his son so I knew he wouldn't take my life. At the end of the day, he did love me, he just never showed it. I can't help but to think maybe he didn't know how to show it, I mean look at me. I treated Lynique horrible for years because I thought it was normal. It took losing her for me to wake up and realize that was no way to show a person you love how you feel.

I got in my rental and headed for the airstrip. I needed to hurry and get to my wife. I have a bad feeling that she lost the baby she was carrying but as long as she was good as well as Jr, we can work on another baby when she was ready.

I had my cousin Trell meet with me at the airport in Boston so that I could get right to my wife. On the way to the hospital it was quiet for awhile before he spoke up.

"What you going to do now with the streets fam?" Trell asked me.

"Honestly, I don't have anything in stone just yet. Once I get this shit with my wife taken care of I'm going to call a meeting with everyone. I have some things to discuss, but yo, do you think now that you older your pops will let you get some real weight and do your thing?" I asked him.

You see, his father and mine was brothers. I meant what I told Lynique back in Antigua and I was willing to give up the streets and go all the way legal, but I owed my men that been rocking with me for years a way to keep they pockets growing even if I was retiring.

"What you getting at?" Trell asked me.

"Get your hands on the shit and take over. I have a lot of men waiting on that and I'm not fucking with my father. You family so I don't see why they won't let you start getting more money. I'm done with this shit. My wife and son are my focus now."

"Just like that, you giving up your business for a bitch that ran off for 5 years with your son, she drops some pussy on you, you get married and now its fuck the streets? I don't get it cuz."

"It's not for you to get! Speak on my wife again and your father won't find your body. You my family but that don't mean you get a free pass at talking bout what you don't know. You lived a good life here in the states with your father, you learned how to love. Lynique is who showed me what love was and how it should be treated, and it took her leaving for those years with my son for me to wake the hell up."

"Damn, my bad, I ain't realize it was such a sensitive topic. Let me get you to this damn hospital." Trell said.

"Like I said you ain't got to worry bout me, I'm still that nigga. Are you going to get with Unc or my pops or you want me to get at your father bout getting you up and running?" I asked him.

"From the sounds of your trip and seeing the stress lines etched on your face, I think it would be best if I holla at them."

"Bet." I answered.

CHAPTER SEVENTEEN

Lynique

"You weren't here baby? You promised me you would always be by my side if I needed you! I needed you Damon, but you were too busy taking care of the streets and not me." I cried out of frustration when Damon walked into my hospital room.

"I came as soon as your brother called me." he told me.

"So, he could suddenly get ahold of you but when I asked him on the phone he said he ain't heard from you? Fuck out of here and tell his ass to leave too while you're at it." I spat. I was hurt, no that was an understatement. I was so happy when I found out I was pregnant, happy that this time around my child's father would be at the appointments with me. Sharing in the excitement. Hearing the heartbeat for the first time, feeling the baby kick. Even holding my

161

hair up for me when I was sick with my head in a toilet or rubbing my swollen feet. Now I don't know if that will ever happen. I'm not sure if having anymore babies with a man so devoted to the streets will be smart. I lost my baby when that car ran that red light and crashed into me. I'm glad that Jr wasn't really hurt. They were releasing him to Damon today. He only had some bumps and bruises. The impact of the airbag and the stress I was already under is the reason for me having the miscarriage.

"You can't keep doing that baby. You either run or try to push people away. I'm just as much hurt over you losing the baby but what you ain't going to do is take your pain out on me. I lost that baby as well." Damon said, taking a seat and not listening to my request of him leaving.

"You don't know what it feels like, so I have every right to be mad."

"Mad, yes. Mad at the careless person who ran the light and crashed into you but mad at me or your brother no. I went to fucking tell my father I was out the business, I walked away from my father and rushed home when I heard you went out the house at night while emotional, not thinking with a clear head. You should have kept your ass home and maybe you wouldn't be laying in this bed but do you see me blaming you no. Accidents happen Lynique. Together we will get thru this and when the time is right, we will be hard at work making another baby. You ain't getting rid of me nor will you keep running." Damon stated while holding my face in his hands making me look directly at him as he spoke.

I guess he put me in my place. I just broke down. I harbor way too much pain and hate. He has shown me repeatedly he loves me. He has put me and Jr first since I revealed having his kid, yet I have pushed and not fully embraced the fact that I have an amazing man who has changed his life for his family. I can't believe he is leaving

162

the streets alone, but I have to admit, it made me feel good inside.

"Lynique baby, I want you to get all those tears the hell out. The anger, along with the sad. I don't want you to feel any of those feelings ever again. It's been a week today I made vows to love you forever and that is what I am going to do. You won't have to worry bout anything ever again. Do you not only hear me but understand what I am saying?"

Barely able to speak from the emotions taking over me I was able to muster up a response, "I more than understand, I believe you."

With that he leaned in and kissed me. I guess he was right, we can try for another baby. Its crazy how he can just speak a few words and take control of my mind. Before he spoke I was set on not having another baby, now unbeknown to him I couldn't wait to go home and start working on another one. He is right that I need to let go of all the anger and hurt. He isn't the man I ran from all those years ago, he is the man I fell in love with, the man I can't help but keep on loving. We made it past the ugly and now it will be nothing but sunshine and rainbows for us and I was ready.

THE END